THOMAS
THE TANK ENGINE

• COLLECTION •

THE REV. W. AWDRY

THOMAS
THE TANK ENGINE
• COLLECTION •
THE REV. W. AWDRY

**A UNIQUE COLLECTION OF ENGINE STORIES
FROM *THE RAILWAY SERIES***

DEAN

First published in Great Britain 1998
This edition published in 2002 by Dean,
an imprint of Egmont Books Limited
239 Kensington High Street, London W8 6SA

Thomas the Tank Engine & Friends

A BRITT ALLCROFT COMPANY PRODUCTION

Based on The Railway Series by The Rev W Awdry

Printed and bound in Italy

CONTENTS

THOMAS
the Tank Engine

In which Thomas rescues James,

races Bertie and finally settles down

on his own branch line . . .

THOMAS AND GORDON

THOMAS was a tank engine who lived at a Big Station. He had six small wheels, a short stumpy funnel, a short stumpy boiler, and a short stumpy dome.

He was a fussy little engine, always pulling coaches about. He pulled them to the station ready for the big engines to take out on long journeys; and when trains came in, and the people had got out, he would pull the empty coaches away, so that the big engines could go and rest.

He was a cheeky little engine, too. He thought no engine worked as hard as he did. So he used to play tricks on them. He liked best of all to come quietly beside a big engine dozing on a siding and

make him jump.

"Peep, peep, peep, pip, peep! Wake up, lazybones!" he would whistle, "why don't you work hard like me?"

Then he would laugh rudely and run away to find some more coaches.

One day Gordon was resting on a siding. He was very tired. The big Express he always pulled had been late, and he had had to run as fast as he could to make up for lost time.

He was just going to sleep when Thomas came up in his cheeky way.

"Wake up, lazybones," he whistled, "do some hard work for a change – you can't catch me!" and he ran off laughing.

Instead of going to sleep again, Gordon thought how he could pay Thomas out.

One morning Thomas wouldn't wake up. His Driver and Fireman couldn't make him start. His fire went out and there was not enough steam.

It was nearly time for the Express. The people were waiting, but the coaches weren't ready.

At last Thomas started. "Oh, dear! Oh, dear!" he yawned.

"Come on," said the coaches. "Hurry up." Thomas gave them a rude bump, and started for the station.

"Don't stop dawdling, don't stop dawdling," he grumbled.

"Where have you been? Where have you been?" asked the coaches crossly.

Thomas fussed into the station where Gordon was waiting.

"Poop, poop, poop. Hurry up, you," said Gordon crossly.

"Peep, pip, peep. Hurry yourself," said cheeky Thomas.

"Yes," said Gordon, "I will," and almost before the coaches had stopped moving Gordon came out of his siding and was coupled to the train.

"Poop, poop," he whistled. "Get in quickly, please." So the people got in quickly, the signal went down, the clock struck the

hour, the guard waved his green flag, and Gordon was ready to start.

Thomas usually pushed behind the big trains to help them start. But he was always uncoupled first, so that when the train was running nicely he could stop and go back.

This time he was late, and Gordon started so quickly that they forgot to uncouple Thomas.

"Poop, poop," said Gordon.

"Peep, peep, peep," whistled Thomas.

"Come on! Come on!" puffed Gordon to the coaches.

"Pull harder! Pull harder!" puffed Thomas to Gordon.

The heavy train slowly began to move out of the station.

The train went faster and faster; too fast for Thomas. He wanted to stop but he couldn't.

"Peep! Peep! Stop! Stop!" he whistled.

"Hurry, hurry, hurry," laughed Gordon in front.

"You can't get away. You can't get away," laughed the coaches.

Poor Thomas was going faster than he had ever gone before. He was out of breath and his wheels hurt him, but he had to go on.

"I shall never be the same again," he thought sadly, "My wheels will be quite worn out."

At last they stopped at a station. Everyone laughed to see Thomas puffing and panting behind.

They uncoupled him, put him on to a turntable and then he ran on a siding out of the way.

"Well, little Thomas," chuckled Gordon as he passed, "now you know what hard work means, don't you?"

Poor Thomas couldn't answer, he had no breath. He just puffed slowly away to rest, and had a long, long drink.

He went home very slowly and was careful afterwards never to be cheeky to Gordon again.

THOMAS'S TRAIN

THOMAS often grumbled because he was not allowed to pull passenger trains.

The other engines laughed. "You're too impatient," they said. "You'd be sure to leave something behind!"

"Rubbish," said Thomas, crossly. "You just wait, I'll show you."

One night he and Henry were alone. Henry was ill. The men worked hard, but he didn't get better.

Now Henry usually pulled the first train in the morning, and Thomas had to get his coaches ready.

"If Henry is ill," he thought, "perhaps I shall pull his train."

Thomas ran to find the coaches.

"Come *along*. Come *along*," he fussed.

"There's plenty of time, there's plenty of time," grumbled the coaches.

He took them to the platform, and wanted to run round in front at once. But his Driver wouldn't let him.

"Don't be impatient, Thomas," he said.

So Thomas waited and waited. The people got in, the Guard and Stationmaster walked up and down, the porters banged the doors, and still Henry didn't come.

Thomas got more and more excited every minute.

The Fat Director came out of his office to see what was the matter, and the Guard and the Stationmaster told him about Henry.

"Find another engine," he ordered.

"There's only Thomas," they said.

"You'll have to do it then, Thomas. Be quick now!"

So Thomas ran round to the front and backed down on the coaches ready to start.

"Don't be impatient," said his Driver. "Wait till everything is ready."

But Thomas was too excited to listen to a word he said.

What happened then no one knows. Perhaps they forgot to couple Thomas to the train; perhaps Thomas was too impatient to wait till they were ready; or perhaps his Driver pulled the lever by mistake.

Anyhow, Thomas started. People shouted and waved at him but he didn't stop.

"They're waving because I'm such a splendid engine," he thought importantly. "Henry says it's hard to pull trains, but *I* think it's easy."

"Hurry! Hurry! Hurry!" he puffed, pretending to be like Gordon.

As he passed the first signal box, he saw the men leaning out waving and shouting.

"They're pleased to see me," he thought. "They've never seen *me* pulling a train before – it's nice of them to wave," and he whistled, "Peep, peep, thank you," and hurried on.

But he came to a signal at "Danger".

"Bother!" he thought. "I must stop, and I was going so nicely, too. What a

nuisance signals are!" And he blew an angry "Peep, peep" on his whistle.

One of the Signalmen ran up. "Hullo, Thomas!" he said. "What are you doing here?"

"I'm pulling a train," said Thomas proudly. "Can't you *see*?"

"Where are your coaches, then?"

Thomas looked back. "Why bless me," he said, "if we haven't left them behind!"

"Yes," said the Signalman, "you'd better go back quickly and fetch them."

Poor Thomas was so sad he nearly cried.

"Cheer up!" said his Driver. "Let's go back quickly, and try again."

At the station all the passengers were talking at once.

They were telling the Fat Director, the Stationmaster and the Guard what a bad railway it was.

But when Thomas came back and they saw how sad he was, they couldn't be cross. So they coupled him to the train, and this time he *really* pulled it.

But for a long time afterwards the other engines laughed at Thomas, and said:

"Look, there's Thomas, who wanted to pull a train, but forgot about the coaches!"

THOMAS AND THE TRUCKS

THOMAS used to grumble in the Shed at night.

"I'm tired of pushing coaches, I want to see the world."

The others didn't take much notice, for Thomas was a little engine with a long tongue.

But one night, Edward came to the shed. He was a kind little engine, and felt sorry for Thomas.

"I've got some trucks to take home tomorrow," he told him. "If you take them instead, I'll push coaches in the Yard."

"Thank you," said Thomas, "that will be nice."

So they asked their Drivers next morning, and when they said "Yes,"

Thomas ran happily to find the trucks.

Now trucks are silly and noisy. They talk a lot and don't attend to what they are doing. They don't listen to their engine, and when he stops they bump into each other screaming.

"Oh! Oh! Oh! Oh! Whatever is happening?"

And, I'm sorry to say, they play tricks on an engine who is not used to them.

Edward knew all about trucks. He warned Thomas to be careful, but Thomas was too excited to listen.

The shunter fastened the coupling, and, when the signal dropped, Thomas was ready.

The Guard blew his whistle. "Peep! Peep!" answered Thomas and started off.

But the trucks weren't ready.

"Oh! Oh! Oh! Oh!" they screamed as their couplings tightened. "Wait, Thomas, wait." But Thomas wouldn't wait.

"Come — on; come — on," he puffed, and the trucks grumbled slowly out of the siding on to the main line.

Thomas was happy. "Come along. Come along," he puffed.

"All — right! — don't — fuss — all — right! — don't fuss," grumbled the trucks. They clattered through stations, and rumbled over bridges.

Thomas whistled "Peep! Peep!" and they rushed through the tunnel in which Henry had been shut up.

Then they came to the top of the hill where Gordon had stuck.

"Steady now, steady," warned the driver, and he shut off steam, and began to put on the brakes.

"We're stopping, we're stopping," called Thomas.

"No! No! No! No!" answered the trucks, and

bumped into each other. "Go — on! — go — on!" and before his driver could stop them, they had pushed Thomas down the hill, and were rattling and laughing behind him.

Poor Thomas tried hard to stop them from making him go too fast.

"Stop pushing, stop pushing," he hissed, but the trucks would not stop.

"Go — on! — go — on!" they giggled in their silly way.

He was glad when they got to the bottom. Then he saw in front the place where they had to stop.

"Oh, dear! What shall I do?"

They rattled through the station, and luckily the line was clear as they swerved into the goods yard.

"Oo ——————— ooh e ——————— r," groaned Thomas, as his brakes held fast and he skidded along the rails.

"I must stop," and he shut his eyes tight.

When he opened them he saw he had stopped just in front of the buffers, and there watching him was ———

The Fat Director!

"What are *you* doing here, Thomas?" he asked sternly.

"I've brought Edward's trucks," Thomas answered.

"Why did you come so fast?"

"I didn't mean to, I was *pushed*," said Thomas sadly.

"Haven't you pulled trucks before?"

"No."

"Then you've a lot to learn about trucks, little Thomas.

They are silly things and must be kept in their place. After pushing them about here for a few weeks you'll know almost as much about them as Edward. Then you'll be a Really Useful Engine."

THOMAS AND THE BREAKDOWN TRAIN

EVERY day the Fat Director came to the station to catch his train, and he always said "Hullo" to Thomas.

There were lots of trucks in the Yard – different ones came in every day – and Thomas had to push and pull them into their right places.

He worked hard – he knew now that he wasn't so clever as he had thought. Besides, the Fat Director had been kind to him and he wanted to learn all about trucks so as to be a Really Useful Engine.

But on a siding by themselves were some trucks that Thomas was told he "mustn't touch".

There was a small coach, some flat trucks, and two queer things his Driver called cranes.

"That's the breakdown train," he said. "When there's an accident, the workmen get into the coach, and the engine takes them quickly to help the hurt people, and to clear and mend the line. The cranes are for lifting heavy things like engines, and coaches, and trucks."

One day, Thomas was in the Yard, when he heard an engine whistling "Help! Help!" and a goods train came rushing through much too fast.

The engine (a new one called James) was frightened. His brake blocks were on fire, and smoke and sparks streamed out on each side.

"They're *pushing* me! They're *pushing* me!" he panted.

"On! On! On! On!" laughed the trucks; and still whistling "Help! Help!"

poor James disappeared under a bridge.

"I'd like to teach those trucks a lesson," said Thomas the Tank Engine.

Presently a bell rang in the signal box, and a man came running, "James is off the line – the breakdown train – quickly," he shouted.

So Thomas was coupled on, the workmen jumped into their coach, and off they went.

Thomas worked his hardest. "Hurry! Hurry! Hurry!" he puffed, and this time he wasn't pretending to be like Gordon, he really meant it.

"Bother those trucks and their tricks," he thought, "I hope poor James isn't hurt."

They found James and the trucks at a bend in the line. The brake van and the last few trucks were on the rails, but the front ones were piled in a heap; James was in a field with a cow looking at him, and his Driver and Fireman were feeling him all over to see if he was hurt.

"Never mind, James," they said. "It wasn't your fault, it was those wooden brakes they gave you. We always said they were

no good."

Thomas pushed the breakdown train alongside. Then he pulled the unhurt trucks out of the way.

"Oh —— dear! — oh — dear!" they groaned.

"Serves you right. Serves you right," puffed Thomas crossly.

When the men put other trucks on the line he pulled them away, too. He was hard at work puffing backwards and forwards all the afternoon.

"This'll teach you a lesson, this'll teach you a lesson," he told the trucks, and they answered "Yes — it — will — yes — it — will," in a sad, groany, creaky, sort of voice.

They left the broken trucks and mended the line. Then with two cranes they put James back on the rails. He tried to move but he couldn't, so Thomas helped him back to the Shed.

The Fat Director was waiting anxiously for them.

"Well, Thomas," he said kindly, "I've heard all about it, and I'm very pleased with you. You're a Really Useful Engine.

"James shall have some proper brakes and a new coat of paint, and you —————— shall have a Branch Line all to yourself."

"Oh, Sir!" said Thomas, happily.

Now Thomas is as happy as can be. He has a branch line all to himself, and puffs proudly backwards and forwards with two coaches all day.

He is never lonely, because there is always some engine to talk to at the junction.

Edward and Henry stop quite often, and tell him the news. Gordon is always in a hurry and does not stop; but he never forgets to say "Poop, poop" to little Thomas, and Thomas always whistles "Peep, peep" in return.

THOMAS AND THE GUARD

ILLUSTRATED BY C. REGINALD DALBY

THOMAS the Tank Engine is very proud of his branch line. He thinks it is the most important part of the whole railway.

He has two coaches. They are old, and need new paint, but he loves them very much. He calls them Annie and Clarabel. Annie can only take passengers, but Clarabel can take passengers, luggage and the Guard.

As they run backwards and forwards along the line, Thomas sings them little songs, and Annie and Clarabel sing too.

When Thomas starts from a station he sings, "Oh, come along! We're rather late. Oh, come along! We're rather late." And the coaches sing, "We're coming along, we're coming along."

They don't mind what Thomas says to them because they know he is trying to please the Fat Controller; and they know, too, that if Thomas is cross, he is not cross with them.

He is cross with the engines on the Main Line who have made him late.

One day they had to wait for Henry's train. It was late. Thomas was getting crosser and crosser. "How can I run my line properly if Henry is always late? He doesn't realize that the Fat Controller depends on ME," and he whistled impatiently.

At last Henry came.

"Where have you been, lazybones?" asked Thomas crossly.

"Oh dear, my system is out of order; no one understands my case. You don't know what I suffer," moaned Henry.

"Rubbish!" said Thomas, "you're too fat; you need exercise!"

Lots of people with piles of luggage got out of Henry's train, and they all climbed into Annie and Clarabel. Thomas had to wait till they were ready. At last the Guard blew his whistle, and Thomas started at once.

The Guard turned round to jump into his van, tripped over an old lady's umbrella, and fell flat on his face.

By the time he had picked himself up, Thomas and Annie and Clarabel were steaming out of the station.

"Come along! Come along!" puffed Thomas, but Clarabel didn't want to come. "I've lost my nice Guard, I've lost my nice Guard," she sobbed. Annie tried to tell Thomas "We haven't a Guard, we haven't a Guard," but he was hurrying, and wouldn't listen.

"Oh, come along! Oh, come along!" he puffed impatiently.

Annie and Clarabel tried to put on their brakes, but they couldn't without the Guard.

"Where is our Guard? Where is our Guard?" they cried. Thomas didn't stop till they came to a signal.

"Bother that signal!" said Thomas. "What's the matter?"

"I don't know," said his Driver. "The Guard will tell us in a minute." They waited and waited, but the Guard didn't come.

"Peep peep peep peep! Where is the Guard?" whistled Thomas.

"We've left him behind," sobbed Annie and Clarabel together. The Driver, the Fireman and the passengers looked, and there was the Guard running as fast as he could along the line, with his flags in one hand and his whistle in the other.

Everybody cheered him. He was very hot, so he sat down and had a drink and told them all about it.

"I'm very sorry, Mr Guard," said Thomas.

"It wasn't your fault, Thomas; it was the old lady's umbrella. Look, the signal is down; let's make up for lost time."

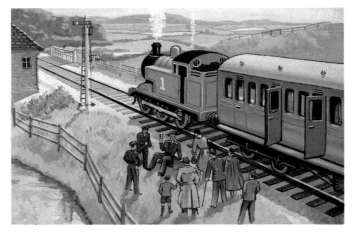

Annie and Clarabel were so pleased to have their Guard again, that they sang, "As fast as you like, as fast as you like!" to Thomas, all the way, and they reached the end of the line quicker than ever before.

THOMAS GOES FISHING

ILLUSTRATED BY C. REGINALD DALBY

THOMAS' branch line had a station by a river. As he rumbled over the bridge, he would see people fishing. Sometimes they stood quietly by their lines; sometimes they were actually jerking fish out of the water.

Thomas often wanted to stay and watch, but his Driver said, "No! what would the Fat Controller say if we were late?"

Thomas thought it would be lovely to stop by the river. "I should like to go fishing," he said to himself longingly.

Every time he met another engine he would say "I want to fish." They all answered "Engines don't go fishing."

"Silly stick-in-the-muds!" he would snort impatiently.

Thomas generally had to take in water at the station by the river. One day he stopped as usual, and his Fireman put the pipe from the water tower in his tank. Then he turned the tap, but it was out of order and no water came.

"Bother!" said Thomas, "I am thirsty." "Never mind," said his Driver, "we'll get some water from the river."

They found a bucket and some rope, and went to the bridge, then the Driver let the bucket down to the water.

The bucket was old, and had five holes, so they had to fill it, pull it up, and empty it into Thomas' tank as quickly as they could.

"There's a hole in my bucket, dear Liza, dear Liza," sang the Fireman.

"Never mind about Liza," said the Driver, "you empty that bucket, before you spill the water over me!"

They finished at last. "That's good! That's good!" puffed Thomas as he started, and Annie and Clarabel ran happily behind.

They puffed along the valley, and were in the tunnel when Thomas began to feel a pain in his boiler, while steam hissed from his safety valve in an alarming way.

"There's too much steam," said his Driver, and his Fireman opened the tap in the feed pipe, to let more water into the boiler, but none came.

"Oh, dear," groaned Thomas, "I'm going to burst! I'm going to burst!"

They damped down his fire, and struggled on.

"I've got such a pain, I've got such a pain," Thomas hissed.

Just outside the last station they stopped, uncoupled Annie and Clarabel and ran Thomas,

who was still hissing fit to burst, on a siding right out of the way.

Then while the Guard telephoned for an Engine Inspector, and the Fireman was putting out the fire, the Driver wrote notices in large letters which he hung on Thomas in front and behind, "DANGER! KEEP AWAY."

Soon the Inspector and the Fat Controller arrived. "Cheer up, Thomas!" they said. "We'll soon put you right."

The Driver told them what had happened. "So the feed pipe is blocked," said the Inspector. "I'll just look in the tanks."

He climbed up and peered in, then he came down. "Excuse me, Sir," he said to the Fat Controller, "please look in the tank and tell me what you see."

"Certainly, Inspector." He clambered up, looked in and nearly fell off in surprise.

"Inspector," he whispered, "can *you* see *fish*?"

"Gracious goodness me!" said the Fat Controller, "how did the fish get there, Driver?"

Thomas' Driver scratched his head, "We must have fished them from the river," and he told them about the bucket.

The Fat Controller laughed, "Well, Thomas, so you and your Driver have been fishing, but fish don't suit you, and we must get them out."

So the Driver and the Fireman fetched rods and nets, and they all took turns at fishing in Thomas' tank, while the Fat Controller told them how to do it.

When they had caught all the fish, the Stationmaster gave them some potatoes, the Driver borrowed a frying-pan, while the Fireman made a fire beside the line and did the cooking.

Then they all had a lovely picnic supper of fish and chips.

"That was good," said the Fat Controller as he finished his share, "but fish don't suit you, Thomas, so you mustn't do it again."

"No, Sir, I won't," said Thomas sadly, "engines don't go fishing, it's too uncomfortable."

THOMAS, TERENCE AND THE SNOW

ILLUSTRATED BY C. REGINALD DALBY

AUTUMN was changing the leaves from green to brown. The fields were changing too, from yellow stubble to brown earth.

As Thomas puffed along, he heard the "chug chug chug" of a tractor at work.

One day, stopping for a signal, he saw the tractor close by.

"Hullo!" said the tractor, "I'm Terence; I'm ploughing."

"I'm Thomas; I'm pulling a train. What ugly wheels you've got."

"They're not ugly, they're caterpillars," said Terence. "I can go anywhere; *I* don't need rails."

"I don't want to go anywhere," said Thomas huffily, "I like my rails, thank you!"

Thomas often saw Terence working, but though he whistled, Terence never answered.

Winter came, and with it dark heavy clouds full of snow.

"I don't like it," said Thomas' Driver. "A heavy fall is coming. I hope it doesn't stop us."

"Pooh!" said Thomas, seeing the snow melt on the rails, "soft stuff, nothing to it!" And he puffed on feeling cold, but confident.

They finished their journey safely; but the country was covered, and the rails were two dark lines standing out in the white snow.

"You'll need your Snow Plough for the next journey, Thomas," said his Driver.

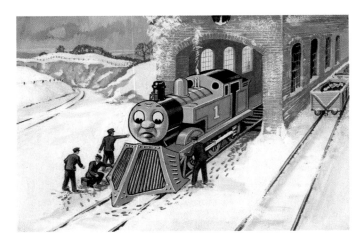

"Pooh! Snow is silly soft stuff – it won't stop me."

"Listen to me," his Driver replied, "we are going to fix your Snow Plough on, and I want no nonsense, please."

The Snow Plough was heavy and uncomfortable and made Thomas cross. He shook it, and he banged it and when they got back it was so damaged that the Driver had to take it off.

"You're a very naughty engine," said his Driver, as he shut the shed door that night.

Next morning, both Driver and Fireman came early and worked hard to mend the Snow Plough; but they couldn't make it fit properly.

It was time for the first train. Thomas was pleased, "I

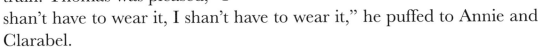

shan't have to wear it, I shan't have to wear it," he puffed to Annie and Clarabel.

"I hope it's all right, I hope it's all right," they whispered anxiously to each other.

The Driver was anxious, too. "It's not bad here," he said to the Fireman, "but it's sure to be deep in the valley."

It was snowing again when Thomas started, but the rails were not covered.

"Silly soft stuff! Silly soft stuff!" he puffed. "I didn't need that stupid old thing yesterday; I shan't today. Snow can't stop me," and he rushed into the tunnel, thinking how clever he was.

At the other end he saw a heap of snow fallen from the sides of the cutting.

"Silly old snow," said Thomas, and charged it.

"Cinders and ashes!" said Thomas, "I'm stuck!" – and he was!

"Back! Thomas, back!" said his Driver. Thomas tried, but his wheels spun, and he couldn't move.

More snow fell and piled up round him.

The Guard went back for help, while the Driver, Fireman and passengers tried to dig the snow away; but, as fast as they dug, more snow slipped down until Thomas was nearly buried.

"Oh, my wheels and coupling rods!" said Thomas sadly, "I shall have to stop here till I'm frozen. What a silly

engine I am," and Thomas began to cry.

At last, a tooting in the distance told them a bus had come for the passengers.

Then Terence chugged through the tunnel.

He pulled the empty coaches away, and came back for Thomas. Thomas' wheels were clear, but still spun helplessly when he tried to move.

Terence tugged and slipped,

and slipped and tugged, and at last dragged Thomas into the tunnel.

"Thank you, Terence, your caterpillars are splendid," said Thomas gratefully.

"I hope you'll be sensible now, Thomas," said his Driver severely.

"I'll try," said Thomas, as he puffed home.

THOMAS AND BERTIE

ILLUSTRATED BY C. REGINALD DALBY

ONE day Thomas was waiting at the junction, when a bus came into the Yard.

"Hullo!" said Thomas, "who are you?"

"I'm Bertie, who are you?"

"I'm Thomas; I run this line."

"So you're Thomas. Ah – I remember now, you stuck in the

snow, I took your passengers and Terence pulled you out. I've come to help you with your passengers today."

"Help me!" said Thomas crossly, going bluer than ever and letting off steam. "I can go faster than you."

"You can't."

"I can."

"I'll race you," said Bertie. Their Drivers agreed. The Stationmaster said, "Are you ready? – Go!" and they were off.

Thomas never could go fast at first, and Bertie drew in front. Thomas was running well but he did not hurry.

"Why don't you go fast? Why don't you go fast?" called Annie and Clarabel anxiously.

"Wait and see, wait and see," hissed Thomas.

"He's a long way ahead, a long way ahead," they wailed, but Thomas didn't mind. He remembered the level crossing.

There was Bertie fuming at the gates while they sailed gaily through.

"Goodbye, Bertie," called Thomas.

The road left the railway and went through a village, so they couldn't see Bertie.

They stopped at the station. "Peep pip peep! Quickly, please!" called Thomas. Everybody got out quickly, the Guard whistled and off they went.

"Come along! Come along!" sang Thomas.

"We're coming along! We're coming along!" sang Annie and Clarabel.

"Hurry! Hurry! Hurry!" panted Thomas, looking straight ahead.

Then he whistled shrilly in horror, for Bertie was crossing the bridge over the railway, tooting triumphantly on his horn!

"Oh, deary me! Oh, deary me!" groaned Thomas.

"He's a long way in front, a long way in front," wailed Annie and Clarabel.

"Steady, Thomas," said his Driver, "we'll beat Bertie yet."

"We'll beat Bertie yet; we'll beat Bertie yet," echoed Annie and Clarabel.

"We'll do it; we'll do it,"

panted Thomas bravely. "Oh, bother, there's a station."

As he stopped, he heard a toot.

"Goodbye, Thomas, you must be tired. Sorry I can't stop, we buses have to work you know. Goodbye!"

The next station was by the river. They got there quickly, but the signal was up.

"Oh, dear," thought Thomas, "we've lost!"

But he felt better after a drink. Then James rattled through with a goods train, and the signal dropped, showing the line was clear.

"Hurrah, we're off! Hurrah, we're off!" puffed Thomas gaily.

As they rumbled over the bridge they heard an impatient "Toot, Toot," and there was Bertie waiting at the red light, while cars and lorries crossed the narrow bridge in the opposite direction.

Road and railway ran up the valley side by side, a stream tumbling between.

Thomas had not crossed the bridge when Bertie started with a roar, and soon shot ahead. Excited passengers in train and bus cheered and shouted across the valley. Now Thomas reached his full speed and foot by foot, yard by yard

he gained, till they were running level. Bertie tried hard, but Thomas was too fast; slowly but surely he drew ahead, till whistling triumphantly he plunged into the tunnel, leaving Bertie toiling far behind.

"I've done it! I've done it," panted Thomas in the tunnel.

"We've done it, hooray! We've done it, hooray!" chanted

Annie and Clarabel; and whistling proudly, they whooooshed out of the tunnel into the last station.

The passengers gave Thomas "three cheers" and told the Stationmaster and the porters all about the race. When Bertie came in they gave him "three cheers" too.

"Well done, Thomas," said Bertie. "That was fun, but to beat you over that hill I should have to grow wings and be an aeroplane."

Thomas and Bertie now keep each other very busy. Bertie finds people in the villages who want to go by train, and takes them to Thomas; while Thomas brings people to the station for Bertie to take home.

They often talk about their race. But Bertie's passengers don't like being bounced like peas in a frying-pan! And the Fat Controller has warned Thomas about what happens to engines who race at dangerous speeds.

So although (between you and me) they would like to have another race, I don't think they ever will.

THE FAT CONTROLLER'S ENGINES

ILLUSTRATED BY JOHN T. KENNEY

ONE evening, Thomas brought his last train to the junction. He went for a drink.

"I'm going to the Big Station," he said to Percy and Toby.

"So are we," they answered.

"Do you know," Percy went on, "I think something's up." Toby looked at the sky, "Where?"

"Down here, silly," laughed Thomas.

"How," asked Toby reasonably, "can something be up when it's down?"

"Look!" said Thomas excitedly, "Look!"

Seven engines from the Other Railway were coming along the line.

"Hullo Jinty!" whistled Percy, "Hullo Pug!

"They're friends of mine," he explained. "I don't know the others."

Jinty and Pug whistled cheerfully as they puffed though the station.

"What *is* all this?" asked Thomas.

"The Fat Controller's got a plan," answered his Driver, "and he's going to tell it to us. Come on."

So they followed to the Big Station at the end of the line where all the engines had gone.

The Fat Controller was waiting for them there.

"The people of England," he said, "read about Us in the Books; but they do not think that we are real. . . ."

"Shame!" squeaked Percy. The Fat Controller glared. Percy subsided.

". . . so," he continued, "I am taking My Engines to England to show them."

"Hooray! Hooray!" the engines whistled.

The Fat Controller held his ears. "Silence!" he bellowed.

"We start the day after tomorrow at 8 a.m. Meanwhile as these engines have kindly come from the Other Railway to take your place, you will show them your work tomorrow."

Next day, as Annie and Clarabel were going to England too, Thomas and Jinty practised with some other coaches.

Thomas was excited. He began boasting about his race with Bertie. "I whooshed through the tunnel and stopped an inch from the buffers. Like this!"

—— CRASH — The buffers broke.

No one was hurt; but Thomas' front was badly bent.

They telephoned the Fat Controller. "I'll send up some men," he said, "but if they can't mend Thomas in time, we'll go to England without him."

Next morning the engines waited at the junction. Toby and Percy were each on a truck and Duck had pushed them into place behind Edward.

Henrietta stood on a siding. The Fat Controller had called her a "curiosity". "I wouldn't dream of leaving you behind," he said, "I'll fit you up

as my private coach." She felt very grand.

Gordon, James and Henry were in front. They whistled impatiently.

The Fat Controller paced the platform. He looked at his watch. "One minute more," he said, turning to the Guard.

"Peep peep peeep!" whistled Thomas and panted into the station.

Annie and Clarabel twittered anxiously. "We hope we're not late; it isn't quite Eight."

"Thomas," said the Fat Controller sternly, "I am most displeased with you. You nearly upset My Arrangements."

Thomas, abashed, arranged himself and the coaches behind Duck, without saying a word!

The Fat Controller climbed into Henrietta. The Guard blew his whistle and waved his flag.

The engines whistled, "Look out England, here we come!" and the cavalcade puffed off.

The engines stood side by side in a big airy shed. Hundreds of people came to see them, and climbed in and out of their cabs every day.

They liked it at first, but

presently felt very bored, and were glad when it was time to go.

The people along their line put the flags out, and cheered them home. "We are glad to see you," they said. "Those others did their best; but they don't know our ways. Nothing anywhere can compare with our Fat Controller's engines."

Thomas Comes to Breakfast

Illustrated by John T. Kenney

Thomas the Tank Engine has worked his Branch Line for many years. "You know just where to stop, Thomas!" laughed his Driver. "You could almost manage without me!"

Thomas had become conceited. He didn't realise his Driver was joking.

"Driver says I don't need him now," he told the others.

"Don't be so daft!" snorted Percy.

"I'd never go without *my* Driver," said Toby earnestly. "I'd be frightened."

"Pooh!" boasted Thomas. "I'm not scared."

"You'd never dare!"

"I would then. You'll see!"

It was dark next morning when the Firelighter came. Thomas drowsed comfortably as the warmth spread through his boiler. He woke again in daylight. Percy and Toby were still asleep. Thomas suddenly remembered. "Silly stick-in-the-muds," he chuckled. "I'll show them! Driver hasn't come yet, so here goes."

He cautiously tried first one piston, then the other. "They're moving! They're moving!" he whispered. "I'll just go out, then I'll stop and 'wheeeeesh'. That'll make them jump!"

Very, very quietly he headed for the door.

Thomas thought he was being clever; but really he was only moving because a careless cleaner had meddled with his controls. He soon found his mistake.

He tried to "wheeeeesh", but he couldn't. He tried to stop, but he couldn't. He just kept rolling along.

"The buffers will stop me," he thought hopefully, but that siding had no buffers. It just ended at the road.

Thomas' wheels left the rails and crunched the tarmac. "Horrors!" he exclaimed, and

shut his eyes. He didn't dare look at what was coming next.

The Stationmaster's family were having breakfast. They were eating ham and eggs.

There was a crash – the house rocked – broken glass tinkled – plaster peppered their plates.

Thomas had collected a bush on his travels. He peered anxiously into the room through its leaves. He couldn't speak. The Stationmaster grimly strode out and shut off steam.

His wife picked up her plate. "You miserable engine," she scolded. "Just look what you've done to our breakfast! Now I shall have to cook some more." She banged the door. More plaster fell. This time, it fell on Thomas.

Thomas felt depressed. The plaster was tickly. He wanted to sneeze, but he didn't dare in case the house fell on him. Nobody came for a long time. Everyone was much too busy.

At last workmen propped up the house with strong poles. They laid rails through the garden, and Donald and Douglas, puffing hard, managed to haul Thomas back to the Yard.

His funnel was bent. Bits of fencing, the bush, and a broken window-frame festooned his front, which was badly twisted. He looked comic.

The Twins laughed and left him. He was in disgrace.

"You are a very naughty engine."

"I know, Sir. I'm sorry, Sir." Thomas' voice was muffled behind his bush.

"You must go to the Works, and have your front end mended. It will be a long job."

"Yes, Sir," faltered Thomas.

"Meanwhile," said the Fat Controller, "a Diesel Rail-car will do your work."

"A D-D-Diesel, Sir?" Thomas spluttered.

"Yes, Thomas. Diesels *always* stay in their sheds till they are wanted. Diesels *never* gallivant off to breakfast in Stationmasters' houses." The Fat Controller turned on his heel, and sternly walked away.

PERCY
the Small Engine

In which Percy gets to wear a "scarf"

and comes to the rescue

by running away . . .

TROUBLE IN THE SHED

ILLUSTRATED BY C. REGINALD DALBY

THE Fat Controller sat in his office and listened. The Fat Controller frowned and said, "What a nuisance passengers are! How can I work with all this noise?"

The Stationmaster knocked and came in, looking worried.

"There's trouble in the Shed, Sir. Henry is sulking; there is no train, and the passengers are saying this is a Bad Railway."

"Indeed!" said the Fat Controller. "We cannot allow that. Will you quieten the passengers, please; I will go and speak to Henry."

He found Henry, Gordon and James looking sulky.

"Come along, Henry," he said, "it is time your train was ready."

"Henry's not going," said Gordon rudely.

"We *won't* shunt like Common Tank Engines. We are Important Tender Engines. You fetch our coaches and we will pull them. Tender Engines don't shunt," and all three engines let off steam in a cheeky way.

"Oh indeed," said the Fat Controller severely. "We'll see about that; engines on My Railway do as they are told."

He hurried away, climbed into his car and drove to find Edward.

"The Yard has never been the same since Thomas left," he thought sadly. Edward was shunting.

"Leave those trucks please, Edward; I want you to push coaches for me in the Yard."

"Thank you, Sir, that will be a nice change."

"That's a good engine," said the Fat Controller kindly, "off you go then."

So Edward found coaches for the three engines, and that day the trains ran as usual.

But when the Fat Controller came next morning, Edward looked unhappy.

Gordon came clanking past, hissing rudely. "Bless me!" said the Fat Controller. "What a noise!"

"They all hiss me, Sir," answered Edward sadly. "They say 'Tender Engines don't shunt', and last night they said I had black wheels. I haven't, have I, Sir?"

"No, Edward, you have nice blue ones, and I'm proud of you. Tender Engines do shunt, but all the same you'd be happier in your own Yard. We need a Tank Engine here."

He went to an Engine Workshop, and they showed him all sorts of Tank Engines. There were big ones, and little ones; some looked happy, and

some sad, and some looked at him anxiously, hoping he would choose them.

At last he saw a smart little green engine with four wheels.

"That's the one," he thought.

"If I choose you, will you work hard?"

"Oh Sir! Yes Sir!"

"That's a good engine; I'll call you Percy."

"Yes Sir! Thank you Sir!" said Percy happily.

So he bought Percy and drove him back to the Yard.

"Edward," he called, "here's Percy; will you show him everything?"

Percy soon learned what he had to do, and they had a happy afternoon.

Once Henry came by hissing as usual.

"Whee ———— eesh!" said Percy suddenly; Henry jumped and ran back to the Shed.

"How beautifully you wheeshed him," laughed Edward. "I can't wheesh like that."

"Oh!" said Percy modestly, "that's nothing; you should hear them in the workshop. You have to wheesh loudly to make yourself heard."

Next morning Thomas arrived. "The Fat Controller sent for me; I expect he wants help," he said importantly to Edward.

"Sh! Sh! Here he comes."

"Well done Thomas; you've been quick. Listen, Henry, Gordon and James are sulking; they say they won't shunt like Common Tank Engines. So I have shut them up, and I want you both to run the line."

"Common Tank Engines indeed!" snorted Thomas. "We'll show them."

"And Percy here will help too," said the Fat Controller.

"Oh Sir! Yes Sir! Please Sir!" answered Percy excitedly.

Edward and Thomas worked the line. Starting at opposite ends, they pulled the trains, whistling cheerfully to each other as they passed.

Percy sometimes puffed along the branch line. Thomas was anxious, but both Driver and Guard promised to take care of Annie and Clarabel.

There were fewer trains, but the passengers didn't mind; they knew the three other engines were having a Lesson.

Henry, Gordon and James stayed shut in the Shed, and were cold, lonely and miserable. They wished now they hadn't been so silly.

PERCY RUNS AWAY

ILLUSTRATED BY C. REGINALD DALBY

HENRY, Gordon and James were shut up for several days. At last the Fat Controller opened the Shed.

"I hope you are sorry," he said sternly, "and understand you are not so important after all. Thomas, Edward and Percy have worked the Line very nicely. They need a change, and I will let you out if you promise to be good."

"Yes Sir!" said the three engines, "we will."

"That's right, but please remember that this 'no shunting' nonsense must stop."

He told Edward, Thomas and Percy that they could go and play on the Branch Line for a few days.

They ran off happily and found Annie and Clarabel at the junction. The two coaches were so pleased to see Thomas again, and he took them for a run at once. Edward and Percy played with trucks.

"Stop! Stop! Stop!" screamed the trucks as they were pushed into their proper sidings, but the two engines laughed and went on shunting till the trucks were tidily arranged.

Next, Edward took some empty trucks to the Quarry, and Percy was left alone.

Percy didn't mind that a bit; he liked watching trains and being cheeky to the engines.

"Hurry! Hurry! Hurry!" he would call to them. Gordon, Henry and James got very cross!

After a while he took some trucks over the Main Line to another siding. When they were tidy, he ran on to the Main Line again, and waited for the Signalman to set the points so that he could cross back to the Yard.

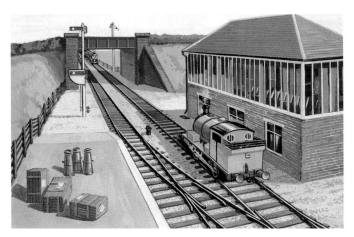

Edward had warned Percy: "Be careful on the Main Line; whistle to tell the Signalman you are there." But Percy didn't remember to whistle, and the Signalman was so busy, and forgot Percy.

Bells rang in the signal box; the man answered, saying the line was clear, and set the signals for the next train.

Percy waited and waited; the points were still against him. He looked along the Main Line . . . "Peep! Peep!" he whistled in horror for, rushing straight towards him, was Gordon with the Express.

"Poop poop poo-poo-poop!" whistled Gordon. His Driver shut off steam and applied the brakes.

Percy's Driver turned on full steam. "Back Percy! Back!" he urged; but Percy's wheels

wouldn't turn quickly. Gordon was coming so fast that it seemed he couldn't stop. With shut eyes Percy waited for the crash. His Driver and Fireman jumped out.

"Oo —— ooh e —— er!" groaned Gordon. "Get out of my way."

Percy opened his eyes; Gordon had stopped with Percy's buffers a few inches from his own.

But Percy had begun to move. "I — won't — stay — here — I'll — run — a — way," he puffed. He was soon clear of the station and running as fast as he could. He went through Edward's station whistling loudly, and was so frightened that he ran right up Gordon's Hill without stopping.

He was tired then, and wanted to stop, but he couldn't . . . he had no Driver to shut off steam and to apply the brakes.

"I shall have to run till my wheels wear out," he thought sadly. "Oh dear! Oh dear!"

"I — want — to — stop, I — want — to — stop," he puffed in a tired sort of way.

He passed another signal box. "I know just what you want, little Percy," called the man kindly. He set the points, and Percy puffed wearily on to a nice empty siding ending in a big bank of earth.

Percy was too tired now to care where he went. "I — want — to — stop, I — want — to — stop —— I — *have* — stopped!" he puffed thankfully, as his bunker buried itself in the bank.

"Never mind, Percy," said the workmen as they dug him out, "you shall have a drink and some coal, and then you'll feel better."

Presently Gordon arrived.

"Well done Percy, you started so quickly that you stopped a nasty accident."

"I'm sorry I was cheeky," said Percy, "you were clever to stop."

Percy now works in the Yard and finds coaches for the trains. He is still cheeky because he is that sort of engine, but he is always *most* careful when he goes on the Main Line.

PERCY AND THE TROUSERS

ILLUSTRATED BY C. REGINALD DALBY

ON cold mornings Percy often saw workmen wearing scarves.

"My funnel's cold, my funnel's cold!" he would puff; "I want a scarf, I want a scarf."

"Rubbish, Percy," said Henry one day, "engines don't want scarves!"

"Engines with proper funnels do," said Percy in his cheeky way. "You've only got a small one!"

Henry snorted; he was proud of his short, neat funnel.

Just then a train came in and Percy, still puffing "I want a scarf, I want a scarf," went to take the coaches to their siding.

His Driver always shut off steam just outside the station, and Percy would try to surprise the coaches by coming in as quietly as he could.

Two porters were taking some luggage across the line. They had a big load and were walking backwards, to see that none fell off the trolley.

Percy arrived so quietly that the porters didn't hear him till the trolley was on the line. The porters jumped clear. The trolley disappeared with a crunch.

Boxes and bags burst in all directions.

"Oo —— ooh e —— r!" groaned Percy and stopped. Sticky streams of red and yellow jam trickled down his face. A top hat hung on his lamp-iron. Clothes, hats, boots, shoes, skirts and blouses stuck to his front. A pair of striped trousers coiled lovingly round his funnel. They were grey no longer!

This story is adapted from one told by Mr. C. Hamilton Ellis in *The Trains We Loved*. We gratefully acknowledge his permission to use it.

Angry passengers looked at their broken trunks. The Fat Controller seized the top hat.

"Mine!" he said crossly.

"Percy," he shouted, "look at this."

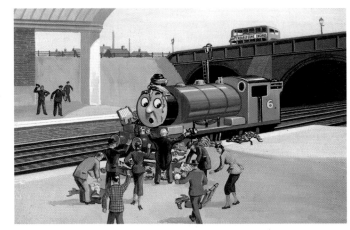

"Yes Sir, I am Sir," a muffled voice replied.

"My best trousers too!"

"Yes Sir, please Sir," said Percy nervously.

"I am very cross," said the Fat Controller. "We must pay the passengers for their spoilt clothes. My hat is dented, and my trousers are ruined, all because you *will* come into the station as if you were playing 'Grandmother's Steps' with the coaches."

The Driver unwound the trousers.

The Fat Controller waved them away.

"Percy wanted a scarf; he shall have my trousers for a scarf; they will keep him warm."

Percy wore them back to the Yard.

He doesn't like scarves now!

PERCY AND THE SIGNAL

ILLUSTRATED BY C. REGINALD DALBY

PERCY is a little green tank engine who works in the Yard at the Big Station. He is a funny little engine, and loves playing jokes. These jokes sometimes get him into trouble.

"Peep peep!" he whistled one morning. "Hurry up, Gordon! The train's ready."

Gordon thought he was late and came puffing out.

"Ha ha!" laughed Percy, and showed him a train of dirty coal trucks.

Gordon didn't go back to the Shed.

He stayed on a siding thinking how to pay Percy out.

"Stay in the Shed today," squeaked Percy to James. "The Fat Controller will come and see you."

James was a conceited engine. "Ah!" he thought, "the Fat Controller knows I'm a fine engine, ready for anything. He wants me to pull a Special train."

So James stayed where he was, and nothing his Driver and Fireman could do would make him move.

But the Fat Controller never came, and the other engines grumbled dreadfully.

They had to do James' work as well as their own.

At last an Inspector came. "Show a wheel, James," he said crossly. "You can't stay here all day."

"The Fat Controller told me to stay here," answered James sulkily. "He sent a message this morning."

"He did not," retorted the Inspector. "How could he? He's away for a week."

"Oh!" said James. "Oh!" and he came quickly out of the Shed. "Where's Percy?" Percy had wisely disappeared!

When the Fat Controller came back, he *did* see James, and Percy too. Both engines wished he hadn't!

James and Gordon wanted to pay Percy out; but Percy kept out of their way. One morning, however, he was so excited that he forgot to be careful.

"I say, you engines," he bubbled, "I'm to take some trucks to Thomas' Junction. The Fat Controller chose me specially. He must know I'm a Really Useful Engine."

"More likely he wants you out of the way," grunted James.

But Gordon gave James a wink. . . . Like this.

"Ah yes," said James, "just so. . . . You were saying, Gordon . . . ?"

"James and I were just speaking about signals at the junction. We can't be too careful about signals. But then, I needn't say that to a Really Useful Engine like you, Percy."

Percy felt flattered.

"Of course not," he said.

"We had spoken of 'backing signals'," put in James. "They need extra special care, you know. Would you like me to explain?"

"No thank you, James," said Percy airily. "I know all about signals," and he bustled off importantly.

James and Gordon solemnly exchanged winks!

Percy was a little worried as he set out.

"I wonder what 'backing signals' are?" he thought.

"Never mind, I'll manage. I know all about signals." He puffed crossly to his trucks, and felt better.

He saw a signal just outside the station. "Bother!" he said. "It's at 'danger'."

"Oh! Oh! Oh!" screamed the trucks as they bumped into each other.

Presently the signal moved to show "line clear". Its arm moved up instead of down. Percy had never seen that sort of signal before. He was surprised.

" 'Down' means 'go'," he thought, "and 'up' means 'stop', so 'upper still' must mean 'go back'. I know! It's one of those 'backing signals'. How clever of me to find that out."

"Come on, Percy," said his Driver, "off we go."

But Percy wouldn't go forward, and his Driver had to let him "back" in order to start at all.

"I am clever," thought Percy, "even my Driver doesn't know about 'backing signals'," and he started so suddenly that the trucks screamed again.

"Whoah! Percy," called his Driver. "Stop! You're going the wrong way."

"But it's a 'backing signal'," Percy protested, and told him about Gordon and James. The Driver laughed, and explained about signals that point up.

"Oh dear!" said Percy, "let's start quickly before they come and see us."

But he was too late. Gordon swept by with the Express, and saw everything.

The big engines talked about signals that night. They thought the subject was funny. They laughed a lot. Percy thought they were being very silly!

Duck Takes Charge

ILLUSTRATED BY C. REGINALD DALBY

"Do you know what?" asked Percy.

"What?" grunted Gordon.

"Do you know what?"

"Silly," said Gordon crossly, "of course I don't know what, if you don't tell me what what is."

"The Fat Controller says that the work in the Yard is too heavy for me. He's getting a bigger engine to help me."

"Rubbish!" put in James. "Any engine could do it," he went on grandly. "If you worked more and chattered less, this Yard would be a sweeter, a better, and a happier place."

Percy went off to fetch some coaches.

"That stupid old signal," he thought, "no one listens to me now. They think I'm a silly little engine, and order me about.

"I'll show them! I'll show them!" he puffed as he ran about the Yard. But he didn't know how.

Things went wrong, the coaches and trucks behaved badly and by the end of the afternoon he felt tired and unhappy.

He brought some coaches to the station, and stood panting at the end of the platform.

"Hullo Percy!" said the Fat Controller, "you look tired."

"Yes, Sir, I am, Sir; I don't know if I'm standing on my dome or my wheels."

"You look the right way up to me," laughed the Fat Controller. "Cheer up!

The new engine is bigger than you, and can probably do the work alone. Would you like to help build my new harbour at Thomas' Junction? Thomas and Toby will help; but I need an engine there all the time."

"Oh yes, Sir, thank you, Sir!" said Percy happily.

The new engine arrived next morning.

"What is your name?" asked the Fat Controller kindly.

"Montague, Sir; but I'm usually called 'Duck'. They say I waddle; I don't really, Sir, but I like 'Duck' better than Montague."

"Good!" said the Fat Controller. " 'Duck' it shall be. Here Percy, come and show 'Duck' round."

The two engines went off together. At first the trucks played tricks, but soon found that playing tricks on Duck was a mistake! The coaches behaved well, though James, Gordon and Henry did not.

They watched Duck quietly doing his work. "He seems a simple sort of engine," they whispered, "we'll have some fun.

"Quaa-aa-aak! Quaa-aa-aak!" they wheezed as they passed him.

Percy was cross; but Duck took no notice. "They'll get tired of it soon," he said.

Presently the three engines began to order Duck about.

Duck stopped. "Do they tell you to do things, Percy?" he asked.

"Yes they do," answered Percy sadly.

"Right," said Duck, "we'll soon stop *that* nonsense." He whispered something . . . "We'll do it tonight."

The Fat Controller had had a good day. There had been no grumbling passengers, all the trains had run to time, and Duck had worked well in the Yard.

The Fat Controller was looking forward to hot buttered toast for tea at home.

He had just left the office when he heard an extraordinary noise. "Bother!" he said, and hurried to the Yard.

Henry, Gordon and James were Wheeeeeshing and snorting furiously; while Duck and Percy calmly sat on the points outside the Shed, refusing to let the engines in.

"STOP THAT NOISE," he bellowed.

"Now Gordon."

"They won't let us in," hissed the big engine crossly.

"Duck, explain this behaviour."

"Beg pardon, Sir, but I'm a Great Western Engine. We Great Western Engines do our work without Fuss; but we are *not* ordered about by other engines. You, Sir, are our

Controller. We will of course move if you order us; but, begging your pardon, Sir, Percy and I would be glad if you would inform these – er – engines that we only take orders from you."

The three big engines hissed angrily.

"SILENCE!" snapped the Fat Controller. "Percy and Duck, I am pleased with your work today; but *not* with your behaviour tonight. You have caused a Disturbance."

Gordon, Henry and James sniggered. They stopped suddenly when the Fat Controller turned on them. "As for you," he thundered, "you've been worse. You made the Disturbance. Duck is quite right. This is My Railway, and I give the orders."

When Percy went away, Duck was left to manage alone.

He did so . . . easily!

PERCY AND HAROLD

ILLUSTRATED BY C. REGINALD DALBY

PERCY worked hard at the harbour. Toby helped, but sometimes the loads of stone were too heavy, and Percy had to fetch them for himself. Then he would push the trucks along the quay to where the workmen needed the stone for their building.

An airfield was close by, and Percy heard the aeroplanes zooming overhead all day. The noisiest of all was a helicopter, which hovered, buzzing like an angry bee.

"Stupid thing!" said Percy, "why can't it go and buzz somewhere else?"

One day Percy stopped near the airfield. The helicopter was standing quite close.

"Hullo!" said Percy, "who are you?"

"I'm Harold, who are you?"

"I'm Percy. What whirly great arms you've got."

"They're nice arms," said Harold, offended. "I can hover like a bird. Don't you wish *you* could hover?"

"Certainly not; I like my rails, thank you."

"I think railways are slow," said Harold in a bored voice.

"They're not much use, and quite out of date." He whirled his arms and buzzed away.

Percy found Toby at the Top Station arranging trucks.

"I say, Toby," he burst out, "that Harold, that stuck-up whirlibird thing, says I'm slow and out of date. Just let him wait, I'll show him!"

He collected his trucks and started off, still fuming.

Soon above the clatter of the trucks they heard a familiar buzzing.

"Percy," whispered his Driver, "there's Harold. He's not far ahead. Let's race him."

"Yes, let's," said Percy excitedly, and quickly gathering

speed, he shot off down the line.

The Guard's wife had given him a flask of tea for "elevenses". He had just poured out a cup when the van lurched and he spilt it down his uniform. He wiped up the mess with his handkerchief, and staggered to the front platform.

Percy was pounding along,

the trucks screamed and swayed, while the van rolled and pitched like a ship at sea.

"Well, I'll be ding-dong-danged!" said the Guard.

Then he saw Harold buzzing alongside, and understood.

"Go it, Percy!" he yelled. "You're gaining."

Percy had never been allowed to run fast before; he was having the time of his life!

"Hurry! Hurry! Hurry!" he panted to the trucks.

"We-don't-want-to; we-don't-want-to," they grumbled; but it was no use, Percy was bucketing along with flying wheels, and Harold was high and alongside.

The Fireman shovelled for dear life, while the Driver was so excited he could hardly keep still.

"Well done, Percy," he shouted, "we're gaining! We're going ahead! Oh good boy, good boy!"

Far ahead, a "distant" signal warned them that the wharf was near. Shut off steam, whistle, "Peep, peep, peep, brakes, Guard, please." Using Percy's brakes too, the Driver carefully checked the train's headlong speed. They rolled under the Main Line, and halted smoothly on the wharf.

"Oh dear!" groaned Percy, "I'm sure we've lost."

The Fireman scrambled to the cab roof. "We've won! We've won!" he shouted and nearly fell off in his excitement.

"Harold's still hovering. He's looking for a place to land!"

"Listen boys!" the Fireman called. "Here's a song for Percy."

Said Harold helicopter to our Percy, "You are slow!
Your Railway is out of date and not much use, you know."
But Percy, with his stone-trucks, did the trip in record time;
And we beat that helicopter on Our Old Branch Line.

The Driver and Guard soon caught the tune, and so did the workmen on the quay.

Percy loved it. "Oh thank you!" he said. He liked the last line best of all.

PERCY'S PROMISE

ILLUSTRATED BY C. REGINALD DALBY

A MOB of excited children poured out of Annie and Clarabel one morning, and raced down to the beach.

"They're the Vicar's Sunday School," explained Thomas. "I'm busy this evening, but the Stationmaster says I can ask you to take them home."

"Of course I will," promised Percy.

The children had a lovely day. But at tea-time it got very hot.

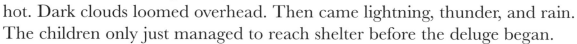

Dark clouds loomed overhead. Then came lightning, thunder, and rain. The children only just managed to reach shelter before the deluge began.

Annie and Clarabel stood at the platform. The children scrambled in.

"Can we go home please, Stationmaster?" asked the Vicar.

The Stationmaster called Percy. "Take the children home quickly please," he ordered.

The rain streamed down on Percy's boiler. "Ugh!" he shivered, and thought of his nice dry shed. Then he remembered.

"A promise is a promise," he told himself, "so here goes."

His Driver was anxious. The river was rising fast. It foamed and swirled fiercely, threatening to flood the country any minute.

The rain beat in Percy's face. "I wish I could see, I wish I could see," he complained.

They left a cutting, and found themselves in water. "Oooh my wheels!"

shivered Percy. "It's cold!" but he struggled on.

"Oooooooooooooshshshshshsh!" he hissed, "it's sloshing my fire."

They stopped and backed the coaches to the cutting and waited while the Guard found a telephone.

He returned looking gloomy.

"We couldn't go back if we wanted," he said, "the bridge near the junction is down."

The Fireman went to the Guard's Van carrying a hatchet.

"Hullo!" said the Guard, "you look fierce."

"I want some dry wood for Percy's fire please."

They broke up some boxes, but that did not satisfy the Fireman. "I'll have some of your floor boards," he said.

"What! My nice floor," grumbled the Guard. "I only swept it this morning," but he found a hatchet and helped.

Soon they had plenty of wood stored in Percy's bunker. His fire burnt well now. He felt warm and comfortable again.

"Buzzzzzzzzzzzzzzzz! Buzzzzzzzzzzzzzzzz! Buzzzzzzzzzzzzzzzz!"

"Oh dear!" thought Percy sadly, "Harold's come to laugh at me."

Bump! Something thudded on Percy's boiler. "Ow!" he exclaimed in a muffled voice, "that's really too bad! He needn't *throw* things."

His driver unwound a parachute from Percy's indignant front.

"Harold isn't throwing things at you," he laughed, "he's dropping hot drinks for us."

They all had a drink of cocoa, and felt better.

Percy had steam up now. "Peep peep! Thank you, Harold!" he whistled. "Come on, let's go."

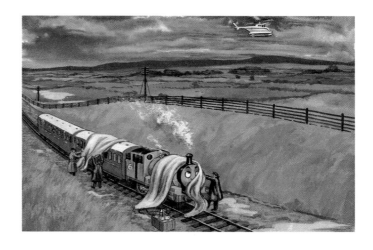

The water lapped his wheels. "Ugh!" he shivered. It crept up and up and up. It reached his ash-pan, then it sloshed at his fire. "Ooooooooooooooshshshshshshshshshshsh!"

Percy was losing steam; but he plunged bravely on. "I promised," he panted, "I promised."

They piled his fire high with wood, and managed to keep him steaming.

"I *must* do it," he gasped, "I must, I must, I must."

He made a last great effort, and stood, exhausted but triumphant, on rails which were clear of the flood.

He rested to get steam back, then brought the train home.

"Three cheers for Percy!" called the Vicar, and the children nearly raised the roof!

The Fat Controller arrived in Harold. First he thanked the men. "Harold told me you were – er – wizard, Percy. He says he can beat you at some things . . ."

Percy snorted.

" . . . but *not* at being a submarine." He chuckled. "I don't know what you've both been playing at, and I won't ask! But I do know that you're a Really Useful Engine."

"Oh Sir!" whispered Percy happily.

PERCY TAKES THE PLUNGE

ILLUSTRATED BY JOHN T. KENNEY

SOMETIMES Percy takes stone trucks to the other end of the line. There, he meets engines from the Other Railway.

One day, Henry wanted to rest in the Shed; but Percy was talking to some tank engines.

". . . It was raining hard. Water swirled under my boiler. I couldn't see where I was going; but I struggled on."

"Ooooh Percy, you *are* brave."

"Well," said Percy modestly, "it wasn't anything really. Water's nothing to an engine with determination."

"Tell us more, Percy," said the engines.

"What are you engines doing here?" hissed Henry. "This shed is for the Fat Controller's Engines. Go away."

"Silly things," Henry snorted.

"They're not silly." Percy had been enjoying himself. He was cross because Henry had sent them away.

"They are silly, and so are you. 'Water's nothing to an engine with determination.' Pah!"

"Anyway," said cheeky

Percy, "I'm not afraid of water. I like it." He ran away singing,

"Once an engine attached to a train
Was afraid of a few drops of rain . . ."

Percy arrived home feeling pleased with himself. "Silly old Henry," he chuckled.

Thomas was looking at a board on the Quay. It said "DANGER".

"We mustn't go past it," he said. "That's Orders."

"Why?"

" 'DANGER' means falling down something," said Thomas. "I went past 'DANGER' once, and fell down a mine."

Percy looked beyond the board. "I can't see a mine," he said.

He didn't know that the foundations of the Quay had sunk, and that the rails now sloped downward to the sea.

"Stupid board!" said Percy. For days and days he tried to sidle past it; but his Driver stopped him every time.

"No you don't," he would say.

Then Percy made a plan.

One day at the Top Station he whispered to the trucks. "Will you give me a bump when we get to the Quay?"

The trucks were surprised. They had never been asked to bump an engine before. They giggled and chattered about it the whole way down.

"Whoah Percy! Whoah!" said his Driver, and Percy checked obediently at the "distant" signal.

"Driver doesn't know my plan," he chuckled.

"On! On! On!" laughed the trucks. Percy thought they were helping. "I'll pretend to stop at the station; but the trucks will push me past the board. Then I'll make them stop. I can do that whenever I like."

If Percy hadn't been so conceited, he would never have been so silly.

Every wise engine knows that you cannot trust trucks.

They reached the station, and Percy's brakes groaned. That was the signal for the trucks.

"Go on! Go on!" they yelled, and surged forward together.

They gave Percy a fearful bump, and knocked his Driver and Fireman off the footplate.

"Ow!" said Percy, sliding past the board.

The day was misty. The rails were slippery. His wheels wouldn't grip.

Percy was frantic. "That's enough!" he hissed.

But it was too late. Once on the slope, he tobogganed helplessly down, crashed through the buffers, and slithered into the sea.

"You are a very disobedient engine."

Percy knew that voice. He groaned.

The Foreman borrowed a small boat and rowed the Fat Controller round.

"Please, Sir, get me out Sir, I'm truly sorry Sir."

"No, Percy, we cannot do that till high tide. I hope it will teach you to obey Orders."

"Yes, Sir," Percy shivered miserably. He was cold. Fish were playing hide and seek through his wheels. The tide rose higher and higher.

He was feeling his position more and more deeply every minute.

It was nearly dark when they brought floating cranes, cleared away the trucks, and lifted Percy out.

He was too cold and stiff to move by himself, so he was sent to the Works next day on Henry's goods train.

"Well! Well! Well!" chuckled Henry, "Did you like the water?"

"No."

"I *am* surprised. You need more determination, Percy. 'Water's nothing to an engine with determination' you know. Perhaps you will like it better next time."

But Percy is quite determined that there won't be a "next time".

PERCY'S PREDICAMENT

ILLUSTRATED BY JOHN T. KENNEY

TOBY brought Henrietta to the Top Station. Percy was grumpily shunting. "Hullo, Percy," he said, "I see Daisy's left the milk again."

"I'll have to make a special journey with it, I suppose," grumbled Percy. "Anyone would think I'd nothing to do."

Toby pondered the problem. "Tell you what," he said at last, "I'll take the milk; you fetch my trucks."

Their Drivers and the Stationmaster agreed, and both engines set off. They thought it would be a nice change.

Percy trundled away to the Quarry. He had never been there before. "It's steep," he thought, "but I can manage. Trucks don't dare to play tricks on me now."

He marshalled them in a lordly way. "Hurry along there," he said, and bumped them if they dallied. The trucks were annoyed.

"This is Toby's place," they grumbled, "Percy's got no right to poke his funnel up here and push us around."

They whispered and passed the word.

"Pay Percy out!"

At last they were all arranged. "Come along," puffed Percy sharply. "No nonsense."

"We'll give him nonsense!" giggled the trucks, but they followed so quietly that Percy thought they were completely under control.

They rumbled along the twisty line till they saw ahead the notice saying ALL TRAINS STOP TO PIN DOWN BRAKES.

"Peep! Peep! Peep!" whistled Percy. "Brakes, Guard, please!" But before he could check them the trucks surged forward. "On! On!" they cried.

Percy, taken by surprise, could not stop them, and in a moment they were careering down the hill.

"Help! Help!" whistled Percy. The man on duty at the street-crossing rushed to warn traffic with his red flag, but was too late to switch Percy to the "runaway" siding.

A slow-moving cockerel lost his tail feathers as Percy thundered across, but Percy couldn't bother with him. He had other things to worry about.

Frantically trying to grip the rails, he slid past the Engine Shed into the Yard, "Peeep peeeeeeep! Look out!" he whistled. His Driver and Fireman jumped clear. Percy shut his eyes and waited for the end.

At the end of the Yard there are sheds where workmen

shape rough stone brought from the Quarry. Then they load it into trucks, which are pulled to another siding out of the way. A train of these stood here when Percy came slithering down.

The Guard had left his van. He was talking to the Stationmaster. They heard frantic whistling and a splintering crash. They rushed from the office.

The brake van was in smithereens. Percy, still whistling fit to burst, was perched on a couple of trucks, while his own trucks were piled up behind him.

The Fat Controller arrived next day. Toby and Daisy had helped to remove most of the wreckage, but Percy still stood on his perch.

"We must now try," said the Fat Controller crossly, "to run the Branch Line with Toby and a Diesel. You have put us in an Awkward Predicament."

"I'm sorry, Sir."

"You can stay there," the Fat Controller went on, "till we are ready. Perhaps it will teach you to be careful with trucks."

Percy sighed. The trucks wobbled beneath his wheels. He quite understood about awkward predicaments.

The Fat Controller spoke severely to Daisy, too.
"My engines do not tell lies," he said. "They work hard, with no shirking. I send lazy engines away."

Daisy was ashamed.

"However," he went on, "Toby says you worked hard yesterday after Percy's accident, so you shall have another chance."

"Thank you, Sir," said Daisy. "I *will* work hard, Sir. Toby says he'll help me."

"Excellent! What Toby doesn't know about Branch Line problems," the Fat Controller chuckled, "such as – er – bulls, isn't worth knowing. Our Toby's an Experienced Engine."

Thomas came back next day, and Percy was sent to be mended. Annie and Clarabel were delighted to see Thomas again, and he took them for a run at once because they hadn't been out while he was away.

Thomas, Toby, and Daisy are now all friends. Daisy often takes the milk for Thomas and when Toby is busy, she takes Henrietta.

Toby has taught Daisy a great deal. She "shooed" a cow off the line all by herself the other day!

That shows you, doesn't it?

GHOST TRAIN

ILLUSTRATED BY GUNVOR AND PETER EDWARDS

". . . AND every year on the date of the accident it runs again, plunging into the gap, shrieking like a lost soul."

"Percy, what *are* you talking about?"

"The Ghost Train. Driver saw it last night."

"Where?" asked Thomas and Toby together.

"He didn't say, but it must have been on our line. He says ghost trains run as a warning to others. "Oooh!" he went on, "it makes my wheels wobble to think of it!"

"Pooh!" said Thomas. "You're just a silly little engine, Percy. I'm not scared."

"Thomas didn't believe in your ghost," said Percy, next morning.

His Driver laughed. "Neither do I. It was a 'pretend' ghost on television."

Percy was disappointed, but he was too busy all day with his stone trucks to think about ghosts. That evening he came back "light engine" from the harbour. He liked running at night. He coasted along without effort, the rails humming cheerfully under his wheels, and signal lights changing to green at his approach.

He always knew just where he was, even in the dark. "Crowe's Farm Crossing," he chuntered happily. "We shan't be long now."

Sam had forgotten that Mr Crowe wanted a load of lime taken to Forty-acre field. When he remembered, it was nearly dark. He drove in a hurry, bumped over the crossing, and sank his cart's front wheels in mud at the field gate.

The horse tried hard, but couldn't move it. The cart's tail still fouled the railway.

Sam gave it up. He unharnessed the horse, and rode back to the farm for help. "There's still time," he told himself. "The next train isn't due for an hour."

But he'd reckoned without Percy. Percy broke the cart to

smithereens, and lime flew everywhere. They found no one at the crossing, so went on to the nearest signal box.

"Hullo!" said the Signalman. "What have you done to Percy? He's white all over!"

Percy's Driver explained. "I'll see to it," said the Signalman, "but you'd better clean Percy, or people will think he's a ghost!"

Percy chuckled. "Do let's pretend I'm a ghost, and scare Thomas. That'll teach him to say I'm a silly little engine!"

On their way they met Toby, who promised to help.

Thomas was being "oiled up" for his evening train, when Toby hurried in saying, "Percy's had an accident."

"Poor engine!" said Thomas. "Botheration! That means I'll be late."

"They've cleared the line for you," Toby went on, "but there's something worse – "

"Out with it, Toby," Thomas interrupted. "I can't wait all evening."

" – I've just seen something," said Toby in a shaky voice. "It *looked* like Percy's ghost. It s-said it w-was c-coming here t-to w – warn us."

"Pooh! Who cares? Don't be frightened, Toby. I'll take care of you."

Percy approached the Shed quietly and glided through it.

"Peeeeep! peeeeeeeeeeeep! pip! pip! pip! Peeeeeeeeeeeeeeeeeeeep!" he shrieked.

As had been arranged, Toby's Driver and Fireman quickly shut the doors.

"Let me in! Let me in!" said Percy in a spooky voice.

"No, no!" answered Toby. "Not by the smoke of my chimney, chim chim!"

"I'll chuff and I'll puff, and I'll break your door in!"

"Oh dear!" exclaimed Thomas. "It's getting late . . . I'd no idea . . . I must find Annie and Clarabel . . ."

He hurried out the other way.

Percy was none the worse for his adventure. He was soon cleaned; but Thomas never returned. Next morning Toby asked him where he'd been.

"Ah well," said Thomas. "I knew you'd be sad about Percy, and – er – I didn't like to – er – intrude. I slept in the Goods Shed, and . . . Oh!" he

went on hurriedly, "sorry . . . can't stop . . . got to see a coach about a train," and he shot off like a jack rabbit.

Percy rolled up alongside. "Well! Well! Well!" he exclaimed. "What d'you know about that?"

"Anyone would think," chuckled Toby, "that our Thomas had just seen a ghost!"

WOOLLY BEAR

ILLUSTRATED BY GUNVOR AND PETER EDWARDS

GANGERS had been cutting the line-side grass and "cocking" it.

The Fat Controller sells the hay to hill-farmers who want winter feed for their stock.

At this time of year, when Percy comes back from the harbour, he stops where they have been cutting. The men load up his empty wagons, and he pulls them to Ffarquhar. Toby then takes them to the hills. The farmers collect the hay from Toby's top station.

When in the wagons, the hay is covered to prevent it blowing about, but on the line-side it is stacked in the open air to dry.

"Wheeeeeeeeeesh!" Percy gave his ghostly whistle. "Don't be frightened, Thomas," he laughed, "it's only me!"

"Your ugly fizz is enough to frighten anyone," said Thomas crossly. "You're like – "

"Ugly indeed! I'm – "

" – a green caterpillar with red stripes," continued Thomas firmly. "You crawl like one too."

"I don't."

"Who's been late every afternoon this week?"

"It's the hay."

"I can't help that," said Thomas. "Time's time, and the Fat Controller relies on me to keep it. I can't if you crawl in the hay till all hours."

"Green caterpillar indeed!" fumed Percy. "Everyone says I'm handsome –

or at least *nearly* everyone. Anyway, my curves are better than Thomas's corners."

He took his trucks to the harbour, and spent the morning shunting. "Thomas says I'm always late," he grumbled. "I'm never late – or at least only a few minutes. What's that to Thomas? He can always catch up time further on."

All the same, he and his Driver decided to start home early. It was most unfortunate that, just before they did, a crate of treacle was upset over him. They wiped the worst off, but he was still sticky when he puffed away.

The wind rose as they puffed along. Soon it was blowing a gale.

"Look at that!" exclaimed his Driver.

The wind caught the piled hay, tossing it up and over the track. The gangers tried to clear it, but more always came.

The line climbed here. "Take a run at it Percy," his Driver advised; so, whistling warningly, Percy gathered speed. But the hay made the rails slippery, and his wheels wouldn't grip. Time after time he stalled with spinning wheels and had to wait till the line

ahead was cleared before he could start again.

The Signalman climbed a telegraph pole, the Stationmaster paced the platform, passengers fussed, and Thomas seethed impatiently.

"Ten minutes late! I warned him. Passengers'll complain, and the Fat Controller . . ."

The Signalman shouted, the Stationmaster stood amazed, the passengers exclaimed and laughed as Percy approached.

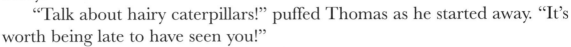

"Sorry – I'm – late!" Percy panted.

"So I should hope," scolded Thomas; but he spoilt the effect as Percy drew alongside. "Look what's crawled out of the hay!" he chortled.

"What's wrong?" asked Percy.

"Talk about hairy caterpillars!" puffed Thomas as he started away. "It's worth being late to have seen you!"

When Percy got home his Driver showed him what he looked like in a mirror.

"Bust my buffers!" exclaimed Percy. "No wonder they all laughed. I'm just like a woolly bear! Please clean me before Toby comes."

But it was no good. Thomas told Toby all about it, and instead of talking about sensible things like playing ghosts, Thomas and Toby made jokes about "woolly bear" caterpillars and other creatures which crawl about in hay.

They laughed a lot, but Percy thought they were really being very silly indeed.

TOBY
the Tram Engine

In which Toby and Henrietta get

a new lease of life when

the Fat Controller comes to stay . . .

TOBY AND THE STOUT GENTLEMAN

ILLUSTRATED BY C. REGINALD DALBY

TOBY is a Tram Engine. He is short and sturdy. He has cow-catchers and side-plates, and doesn't look like a steam engine at all.

He takes trucks from farms and factories to the Main Line, and the big engines take them to London and elsewhere. His tramline runs along roads and through fields and villages. Toby rings his bell cheerfully to everyone he meets.

He has a coach called Henrietta, who has seen better days. She complains because she has few passengers. Toby is attached to Henrietta and always takes her with him.

"She might be useful one day," he says.

"It's not fair at all!" grumbles Henrietta as the buses roar past full of passengers. She remembers that she used to be full, and nine trucks would rattle behind her.

Now there are only three or four, for the farms and factories send their goods mostly by lorry.

Toby is always careful on the road. The cars, buses and lorries often have accidents. Toby hasn't had an accident for years, but the buses are crowded, and Henrietta is empty.

"I can't understand it," says Toby the tram engine.

People come to see Toby, but they come by bus. They stare at him. "Isn't he quaint!" they say, and laugh.

They make him so cross.

One day a car stopped close by, and a little boy jumped out. "Come on Bridget," he called to his sister, and together they ran across to Toby. Two ladies and a stout gentleman followed. The gentleman looked important, but nice.

The children ran back. "Come on grandfather, do look at this engine," and seizing his hands they almost dragged him along.

"That's a tram engine, Stephen," said the stout gentleman.

"Is it electric?" asked Bridget.

"Whoosh!" hissed Toby crossly.

"Sh Sh!" said her brother, "you've offended him."

"But trams *are* electric, aren't they?"

"They are mostly," the stout gentleman answered, "but this is a steam tram."

"May we go in it grandfather? Please!"

The Guard had begun to blow his whistle.

"Stop," said the stout gentleman, and raised his hand. The Guard, surprised, opened his mouth, and the whistle fell out.

While he was picking it up, they all scrambled into Henrietta.

"Hip Hip Hurray!" chanted Henrietta, and she rattled happily behind.

Toby did not sing. "Electric indeed! Electric indeed," he snorted. He was very hurt.

The stout gentleman and his family got out at the junction, but waited for Toby to take them back to their car.

"What is your name?" asked the stout gentleman.

"Toby, Sir."

"Thank you, Toby, for a very nice ride."

"Thank *you*, Sir," said Toby politely. He felt better now. "This gentleman," he thought, "is a gentleman who knows how to speak to engines."

The children came every day for a fortnight. Sometimes they rode with the Guard, sometimes in empty trucks, and on the last day of all the Driver invited them into his cab.

All were sorry when they had to go away.

Stephen and Bridget said "Thank you" to Toby, his Driver, his Fireman, and the Guard.

The stout gentleman gave them all a present.

"Peep pip pip peep," whistled Toby. "Come again soon."

"We will, we will," called the children, and they waved till Toby was out of sight.

The months passed. Toby had few trucks, and fewer passengers.

"Our last day, Toby," said his Driver sadly one morning. "The Manager says we must close tomorrow."

That day Henrietta had more passengers than she could manage. They rode in the trucks and crowded in the brake van, and the Guard hadn't enough tickets to go round.

The passengers joked and sang, but Toby and his Driver wished they wouldn't.

"Goodbye, Toby," said the passengers afterwards, "we are sorry your line is closing down."

"So am I," said Toby sadly.

The last passenger left the station, and Toby puffed slowly to his shed.

"Nobody wants me," he thought, and went unhappily to sleep.

Next morning the shed was flung open, and he woke with a start to see his Fireman dancing a jig outside. His Driver, excited, waved a piece of paper.

"Wake up, Toby," they shouted, "and listen to this; it's a letter from the stout gentleman."

Toby listened and . . .

But I mustn't tell you any more, or I should spoil the next story.

THOMAS IN TROUBLE

ILLUSTRATED BY C. REGINALD DALBY

THERE is a line to a quarry at the end of Thomas' Branch; it goes for some distance along the road.

Thomas was always very careful here in case anyone was coming.

"Peep pip peep!" he whistled; then the people got out of the way, and he puffed slowly along with his trucks rumbling behind him.

Early one morning there was no one on the road, but a large policeman was sitting on the grass close to the line. He was shaking a stone from his boot.

Thomas liked policemen. He had been a great friend of the Constable who used to live in the village; but he had just retired.

Thomas expected that the new Constable would be friendly too.

"Peep peep," he whistled, "good morning."

The policeman jumped and dropped his boot. He scrambled up, and hopped round on one leg till he was facing Thomas.

Thomas was sorry to see that he didn't look friendly at all. He was red in the face and very cross.

The policeman wobbled about, trying to keep his balance.

"Disgraceful!" he spluttered. "I didn't sleep a wink last night, it was so quiet, and now engines come whistling suddenly behind me! My first day in the country too!"

He picked up his boot and hopped over to Thomas.

"I'm sorry, Sir," said Thomas, "I only said 'good morning'."

The policeman grunted, and, leaning against Thomas' buffer, he put his boot on.

He drew himself up and pointed to Thomas.

"Where's your cow-catcher?" he asked accusingly.

"But I don't catch cows, Sir!"

"Don't be funny!" snapped the policeman. He looked at Thomas' wheels. "No side plates either," and he wrote in his notebook.

"Engines going on Public Roads must have their wheels covered, and a cow-catcher in front. You haven't, so you are Dangerous to the Public."

"Rubbish!" said his Driver, "we've been along here hundreds of times and never had an accident."

"That makes it worse," the policeman answered. He wrote "regular lawbreaker" in his book.

Thomas puffed sadly away.

The Fat Controller was having breakfast. He was eating

toast and marmalade. He had the newspaper open in front of him, and his wife had just given him some more coffee.

The butler knocked and came in.

"Excuse me, Sir, you are wanted on the telephone."

"Bother that telephone!" said the Fat Controller.

"I'm sorry, my dear," he said a few minutes later, "Thomas is in trouble with the police, and I must go at once."

He gulped down his coffee and hurried from the room.

At the junction, Thomas' Driver told the Fat Controller what had happened.

"Dangerous to the Public indeed; we'll see about that!" and he climbed grimly into Annie the coach.

The policeman was on the platform at the other end. The Fat Controller spoke to him at once, and a crowd collected to listen.

Other policemen came to see what was happening and the Fat Controller argued with them too; but it was no good.

"The Law is the Law," they said, "and we can't change it."

The Fat Controller felt exhausted.

He mopped his face.

"I'm sorry Driver," he said, "it's no use arguing with policemen. We will have to make those cow-catcher things for Thomas, I suppose."

"Everyone will laugh, Sir," said Thomas sadly, "they'll say I look like a tram."

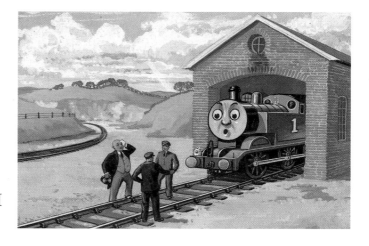

The Fat Controller stared, then he laughed.

"Well done, Thomas! Why didn't I think of it before? We want a tram engine! When I was on my holiday, I met a nice little engine called Toby. He hasn't enough work to do, and needs a change. I'll write to his Controller at once."

A few days later Toby arrived.

"That's a good engine," said the Fat Controller, "I see you've brought Henrietta."

"You don't mind, do you, Sir?" asked Toby anxiously. "The Stationmaster wanted to use her as a hen house, and that would never do."

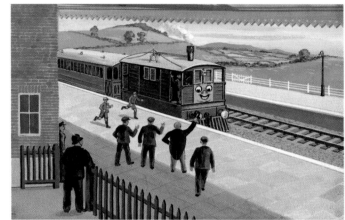

"No, indeed," said the Fat Controller gravely, "we couldn't allow that."

Toby made the trucks behave even better than Thomas did.

At first Thomas was jealous, but he was so pleased when Toby rang his bell and made the policeman jump that they have been firm friends ever since.

DIRTY OBJECTS

ILLUSTRATED BY C. REGINALD DALBY

TOBY and Henrietta take the workmen to the Quarry every morning. At the junction they often meet James.

Toby and Henrietta were shabby when they first came, and needed new paint. James was very rude. "Ugh! What *dirty* objects!" he would say.

At last Toby lost patience.

"James," he asked, "why are you red?"

"I am a splendid engine," answered James loftily, "ready for anything. You never see *my* paint dirty."

"Oh!" said Toby innocently, "that's why you once needed bootlaces; to be ready, I suppose."

James went redder than ever, and snorted off.

At the end of the line James left his coaches and got ready for his next train. It was a "slow goods", stopping at every station to pick up and set down trucks. James hated slow goods trains.

"Dirty trucks from dirty sidings! Ugh!" he grumbled.

Starting with only a few, he picked up more and more

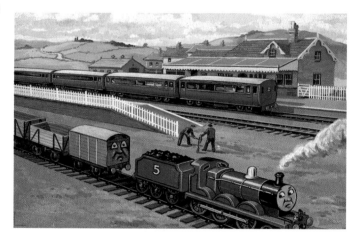

trucks at each station, till he had a long train. At first the trucks behaved well, but James bumped them so crossly that they determined to pay him out.

Presently, rumbling over the viaduct, they approached the top of Gordon's Hill. Heavy goods trains halt here to "pin down" their brakes. James had had an accident with trucks before, and should have remembered this.

"Wait, James, wait," said his Driver, but James wouldn't wait. He was too busy thinking what he would say to Toby when they next met.

Too late he saw where he was, and tried to stop.

"Hurrah! Hurrah!" laughed the trucks, and banging their buffers they pushed him down the hill.

The Guard tightened his brakes until they screamed.

"On! On! On!" yelled the trucks.

"I've *got* to stop, I've *got* to stop," groaned James, and setting his brakes he managed to check the trucks' mad rush, but they were still going much too fast to stop in time.

Through the station they thundered, and lurched into the Yard.

James shut his eyes ——————
There was a bursting crash, and something sticky splashed all over him. He had run into two tar wagons, and was black from smokebox to cab.

James was more dirty than hurt, but the tar wagons and some of the trucks were all to pieces. The breakdown train was in the Yard, and they soon tidied up the mess.

Toby and Percy were sent to help, and came as quickly as they could.

"Look here, Percy!" exclaimed Toby, "whatever is that dirty object?"

"That's James; didn't you know?"

"It's James' shape," said Toby thoughtfully, "but James is a splendid red

engine, and you never see *his* paint dirty."

James shut his eyes, and pretended he hadn't heard.

They cleared away the unhurt trucks, and helped James home.

The Fat Controller met them.

"Well done, Percy and Toby," he said.

He turned to James. "Fancy letting your trucks run away. I *am* surprised. You're not fit to be seen; you must be cleaned at once."

"Toby shall have a coat of paint – chocolate and blue I think."

"Please, Sir, can Henrietta have one too?"

"Certainly Toby," he smiled, "she shall have brown like Annie and Clarabel."

"Oh thank you, Sir! She will be pleased."

Toby ran home happily to tell her the news.

Mrs Kyndley's Christmas

ILLUSTRATED BY C. REGINALD DALBY

It was nearly Christmas. Annie and Clarabel were packed full of people and parcels.

Thomas was having very hard work.

"Come on! Come on!" he puffed.

"We're feeling *so* full!" grumbled the coaches.

Thomas looked at the hill ahead. "Can I do it? Can I do it?" he puffed anxiously.

Suddenly he saw a handkerchief waving from a cottage window. He felt better at once.

"Yes I can, yes I can," he puffed bravely. He pulled his hardest, and was soon through the tunnel and resting in the station.

"That was Mrs Kyndley who waved to you, Thomas," his Driver told him. "She has to stay in bed all day."

"Poor lady," said Thomas, "I am sorry for her."

Engines have heavy loads at Christmas time, but Thomas and Toby didn't mind the hard work when they saw Mrs Kyndley waving.

But then it began to rain. It rained for days and days.

Thomas didn't like it, nor did his Driver.

"Off we go Thomas!" he would say. "Pull hard and get home quickly; Mrs Kyndley won't wave today."

But whether she waved or not, they always whistled when they passed the little lonely cottage. Its white walls stood out against the dark background of the hills.

"Hello!" exclaimed Thomas' Fireman one day. "Look at that!"

The Driver came across the cab. "Something's wrong there," he said.

Hanging flapping and bedraggled from a window of the cottage was something that looked like a large red flag.

"Mrs Kyndley needs help I expect," said the Driver, and put on the brakes. Thomas gently stopped.

The Guard came squelching through the rain up to Thomas's cab, and the Driver pointed to the flag.

"See if a Doctor's on the train and ask him to go to the cottage; then walk back to the station and tell them we've stopped."

The Fireman went to see if the line was clear in front.

Two passengers left the train and climbed to the cottage. Then the Fireman returned.

"We'll back down to the station," said the Driver, "so that Thomas can get a good start."

"We shan't get up the hill," the Fireman answered. "Come and see what's happened!"

They walked along the line round the bend.

"Jiminy Christmas!" exclaimed the Driver, "go back to the train; I'm going to the cottage."

He found the Doctor with Mrs Kyndley.

"Silly of me to faint," she said.

"You saw the red dressing-gown? You're all safe?" asked Mrs Kyndley.

"Yes," smiled the Driver, "I've come to thank you. There was a landslide in the cutting, Doctor, and Mrs Kyndley saw it from her window and stopped us. She's saved our lives!"

"God bless you, ma'am," said the Driver, and tiptoed from the room.

They cleared the line by Christmas Day, and the sun shone as a special train puffed up from the junction.

First came Toby, then Thomas with Annie and Clarabel, and last of all,

but very pleased at being allowed to come, was Henrietta.

The Fat Controller was there, and lots of other people who wanted to say "Thank you" to Mrs Kyndley.

"Peepeep, Peepeep! Happy Christmas!" whistled the engines as they reached the place.

The people got out and climbed to the cottage. Thomas and Toby wished they could go too.

Mrs Kyndley's husband met them at the door.

The Fat Controller, Thomas' Driver, Fireman, and Guard went upstairs, while the others stood in the sunshine below the window.

The Driver gave her a new dressing-gown to replace the one spoilt by the rain. The Guard brought her some grapes, and the Fireman gave her some woolly slippers, and promised to bring some coal as a present from Thomas,

next time they passed.

Mrs Kyndley was very pleased with her presents.

"You are very good to me," she said.

"The passengers and I," said the Fat Controller, "hope you will accept these tickets for the South Coast, Mrs Kyndley, and get really well in the sunshine. We cannot thank you enough for preventing that accident. I hope we have not tired you. Goodbye and a happy Christmas."

Then going quietly downstairs, they joined the group outside the window, and sang some carols before returning to the train.

Mrs Kyndley is now at Bournemouth, getting better every day, and Thomas and Toby are looking forward to the time when they can welcome her home.

DOUBLE HEADER

ILLUSTRATED BY JOHN T. KENNEY

THE Fat Controller gave Gordon a rest when he came back from London. He told James to do his work.

James got very conceited about it.

"You know, little Toby," he said one day, "I'm an Important Engine now; everybody knows it. They come in crowds to see me flash by. The heaviest train makes no difference. I'm as regular as clockwork. They all set their watches by me. Never late, always on time, that's me."

"Sez you," replied Toby cheekily.

Toby was out on the Main Line. The Fat Controller had sent him to the Works. His parts were worn. They clanked as he trundled along.

He was enjoying his journey. He was a little engine, and his tanks didn't hold much water, so he often had to stop for a drink. He had small wheels, too, and he couldn't go fast.

"Never mind," he thought, "the Signalmen all know me; they'll give me plenty of time."

But a new Signalman had come to one of the stations.

Toby had wanted to take Henrietta, but the Fat Controller had said, "No! What would the passengers do without her?"

He wondered if Henrietta was lonely. Percy had promised to look after her; but Toby couldn't help worrying. "Percy doesn't understand her like I do," he said.

He felt thirsty and tired; he had come a long way.

He saw a "distant" signal. "Good," he thought, "now I can have a nice drink, and rest in a siding till James has gone by."

Toby's Driver thought so too. They stopped by the water-crane. His Fireman jumped out and put the hose in his tank.

Toby was enjoying his drink when the Signalman came up. Toby had never seen him before.

"No time for that," said the Signalman. "We must clear the road for the Express."

"Right," said the Driver. "We'll wait in the siding."

"No good," said the Signalman, "it's full of trucks. You'll have to hurry to the next station. They've got plenty of room for you there."

Poor Toby clanked sadly away. "I must hurry! I must hurry!" he panted.

But hurrying used a lot of water, and his tanks were soon empty.

They damped down his fire and struggled on, but he soon ran out of steam, and stood marooned on the Main Line far away from the next station.

The Fireman walked back. He put detonators on the line to warn James and his Driver; then he hurried along the sleepers.

"I'll tell that Signalman something," he said grimly.

James was fuming when Toby's Fireman arrived and explained what had happened.

"My fault," said the Signalman, "I didn't understand about Toby."

"Now James," said his Driver, "you'll have to push him."

"What, me?" snorted James. "ME, push Toby *and* pull my train?"

"Yes, you."

"Shan't."

The Driver, the Firemen, the passengers and the Guard all said he was a Bad Engine.

"All right, all right," grumbled James. He came up behind Toby and gave him a bump.

"Get on you!" he said crossly.

James' Driver made him push Toby all the way to the Works. "It serves you right for being cross," he said.

James had to work very hard and when he reached the Works Station he felt exhausted.

Some little boys ran along the platform. "Coo!" said one, "The Express *is* late. A double header too. Do you know what I think? I think," he went on, "that James couldn't pull the train, so Toby had to help him."

"Cor!" said James and disappeared in a cloud of steam.

MAVIS

ILLUSTRATED BY GUNVOR AND PETER EDWARDS

MAVIS is a diesel engine belonging to the Ffarquhar Quarry Company. They bought her to shunt trucks in their sidings.

She is black, and has six wheels. These, like Toby's, are hidden by sideplates.

Mavis is young, and full of her own ideas. She is sure they are better than anybody else's.

She loves re-arranging things, and put Toby's trucks in different places every day. This made Toby cross.

"Trucks," he grumbled, "should be where you want them, when you want them."

"Fudge!" said Mavis, and flounced away.

At last Toby lost patience. "I can't waste time playing 'Hunt the Trucks' with you," he snapped. "Take 'em yourself."

Mavis was delighted. Taking trucks made her feel important.

At Ffarquhar she met Daisy. "Toby's an old fusspot," she complained.

Daisy liked Toby, but was

glad of a diesel to talk to. "Steam engines," she said, "have their uses, but they don't understand . . ."

"Toby says only steam engines can manage trucks properly . . ."

"What rubbish!" put in Daisy, who knew nothing about trucks. "Depend upon it, my dear, anything steam engines do, we diesels can do better."

Toby's line crosses the main road behind Ffarquhar Station, and, for a short way, follows a farm lane. The rails here are buried in earth and ashes almost to their tops. In wet weather, animals, carts, and tractors make the lane muddy and slippery. Frost makes the mud rock-hard. It swells it too, preventing engine wheels from gripping the rails properly.

Toby found this place troublesome; so, when frost came, he warned Mavis and told her just what to do.

"I can manage, thank you," she said cheekily. "I'm not an old fusspot like you."

The trucks were tired of being pushed around by Mavis. "It's slippery," they whispered. "Let's push *her* around instead."

"On! On! On!" they yelled, as Mavis reached the "Stop" board; but Mavis had heard about Percy, and took no chances. She brought them carefully down to the lane, and stopped at the Level Crossing. There, her Second Man halted the traffic while the Guard unpinned the wagon brakes.

"One in the headlamp for fusspot Toby!" she chortled. She looked forward to having a good giggle about it with Daisy.

But she never got her giggle. She was so sure she was right, that she'd stopped in the wrong place.

In frosty weather Toby stops *before* reaching the lane, and while some of

his trucks are still on the slope. This ensures that they can't hold him back, and their weight helps him forward till his wheels can grip again.

But Mavis had given the trucks the chance they wanted. "Hold back! Hold back!" they giggled.

"Grrrrrrr Up!" ordered Mavis. The trucks just laughed, and her wheels spun helplessly. She tried backing, but the same thing happened.

They sanded the rails, and tried to dig away the frozen mud, but only broke the spade.

Cars and lorries tooted impatiently.

"Grrrrr agh!" wailed Mavis in helpless fury.

"I warned her," fumed Toby. "I told her just where to stop. 'I can manage,' she said, and called me an old fusspot."

"She's young yet," soothed his Driver, "and . . ."

"She can manage her trucks herself."

"They're *your* trucks really," his Driver pointed out. "Mavis isn't supposed to come down here. If the Fat Controller . . ."

"You wouldn't tell, would you?"

"Of course not."

"Well then . . ."

"But," his Driver went on, "if we don't help clear the line, he'll soon know all about it, and so shall we!"

"Hm! Yes!" said Toby thoughtfully.

An angry farmer was telling Mavis just what she could do with her train!

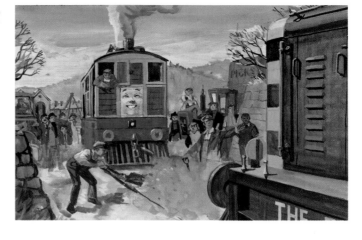

Toby buffered up. "Having trouble, Mavis? I *am* surprised!"

"Grrrrrroosh!" said Mavis.

With much puffing and wheel-slip, Toby pushed the trucks back. Mavis hardly helped at all.

The hard work made Toby's fire burn fiercely. He then reversed, stopping at intervals while his Fireman spread hot cinders to melt the frozen mud. "Goodbye," he called as he reached the crossing. "You'll manage now, I expect."

Mavis didn't answer. She took the trucks to the sheds, and scuttled home as quickly as she could.

TOBY'S TIGHTROPE

ILLUSTRATED BY GUNVOR AND PETER EDWARDS

THE Manager spoke to Mavis severely. "You are a very naughty engine. You have no business to go jauntering down Toby's line instead of doing your work up here."

"It's that Toby," protested Mavis. "He's a fusspot. He . . ."

"Toby has forgotten more about trucks than you will ever know. You will put the trucks where he wants them and nowhere else."

"But . . ."

"There are no 'buts'," said the Manager sternly. "You will do as you are told – or else . . ."

Mavis stayed good for several days!

Mavis soon got tired of being good.

"Why shouldn't I go on Toby's line?" she grumbled. She started making plans.

At the Top Station, the siding arrangements were awkward. To put trucks where Toby wanted them Mavis had to go backwards and forwards taking a few at a time.

"If," she suggested to her Driver, "we used the teeniest bit of Toby's line, we could save all this bother."

Her Driver, unsuspicious, spoke to the Manager, who allowed them to go as far as the first Level Crossing.

Mavis chuckled; but she kept it to herself!

Frost hindered work in the Quarry, but a thaw made them busy again.

More trucks than ever were needed. Some trains were so long that Mavis had to go beyond the Level Crossing.

This gave her ideas, and a chance to go further down the line without it seeming her fault.

"Can you keep a secret?" she asked the trucks.

"Yes! yes! yes!" they chattered.

"Will you bump me at the Level Crossing, and tell no one I asked you?"

The trucks were delighted, and promised.

It was unfortunate that Toby should have arrived while Mavis was elsewhere, and decided to shunt them himself.

They reached the Level Crossing, and Toby's brakes came on. This was the signal for the trucks.

"On! On! On!" they yelled, giving him a fearful bump. His Driver and Fireman, taken unawares, were knocked over in the cab, and before they could pick themselves up, Toby was away, with the trucks screaming and yelling behind him.

What none of them realised was that with the warmer weather melted snow from the mountains had turned a quiet stream into a raging torrent, and that the supports of the bridge they were approaching had already been undermined.

Toby and his crew saw it together. The bridge vanished before their eyes, leaving rails like tightropes stretched across the gap.

"Peep Peep Peeeeep!" whistled Toby.

His Driver, still dazed, fought for control.

Shut regulator – reverser hard over – full steam against the trucks.

"Hold them, boy, hold them. It's up to you."

Nearer and nearer they came. Toby whistled despairingly.

Though their speed was reduced, braking was still risky, but it was all or nothing now. The Driver braked hard. Toby went into a squealing slide, groaned fearfully, and stopped, still on the rails, but with his wheels treading the tightrope over the abyss.

Mavis was horrified. She brought some men who anchored Toby with ropes while she pulled the trucks away. Then she ran to the rescue.

"Hold on, Toby!" she tooted. "I'm coming."

Ropes were fastened between the two engines. Toby still had steam and was able to help, so he was soon safe on firm track, and saying "Thank you" to Mavis.

"I'm sorry about the trucks," said Mavis, "I can't think how you managed to stop them in time."

"Oh, well!" said Toby. "My Driver's told me about circus people who walk tightropes, but I just didn't fancy doing it myself!"

The Fat Controller thanked the Manager and his men for rescuing Toby from his "tightrope".

"A very smart piece of work," he said. "Mavis did well too, I hear."

Mavis looked ashamed. "It was my fault about those trucks, Sir," she faltered. "I didn't know . . . But if I could . . ."

"Could what?" smiled the Fat Controller.

"Come down the line sometimes, Sir. Toby says he'll show me how to go on."

"Certainly, if your Manager agrees."

And so it was arranged. Mavis is now a welcome visitor at Ffarquhar Shed. She is still young and still makes mistakes; but she is never too proud to ask Toby, and Toby always helps her to put things right.

EDWARD
the Blue Engine

In which we meet Edward,

a kind and helpful engine, who finally gets

to see the world . . .

EDWARD'S DAY OUT

ILLUSTRATED BY C. REGINALD DALBY

ONCE upon a time there was a little engine called Edward. He lived in a shed with five other engines. They were all bigger than Edward and boasted about it. "The Driver won't choose you again," they said. "He wants big, strong engines like us." Edward had not been out for a long time; he began to feel sad.

Just then the Driver and Fireman came along to start work.

The Driver looked at Edward. "Why are you sad?" he asked. "Would you like to come out today?"

"Yes, please," said Edward. So the Fireman lit the fire and made a nice lot of steam.

Then the Driver pulled the lever, and Edward puffed away.

"Peep, peep," he whistled. "Look at me now."

The others were very cross at being left behind.

Away went Edward to get some coaches.

"Be careful, Edward," said the coaches, "don't bump and bang us like the other engines do."

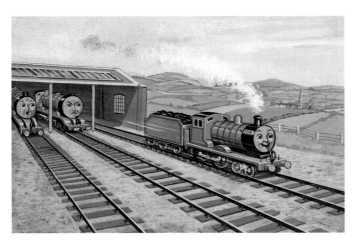

So Edward came up to the coaches, very, very gently, and the shunter fastened the coupling.

"Thank you, Edward," said the coaches. "That was kind, we are glad you are taking us today."

Then they went to the station where the people were waiting.

"Peep, peep," whistled Edward – "get in quickly, please."

So the people got in quickly and Edward waited happily for the Guard to blow his whistle, and wave his green flag.

He waited and waited – there was no whistle, no green flag. "Peep, peep, peep, peep – where is that Guard?" Edward was getting anxious.

The Driver and Fireman asked the Stationmaster, "Have

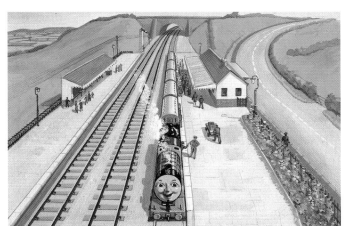

you seen the Guard?" "No," he said. They asked the porter, "Have you seen the Guard?" "Yes – last night," said the porter.

Edward began to get cross. "Are we ever going to start?" he said.

Just then a little boy shouted, "Here he comes!" and there the Guard was, running

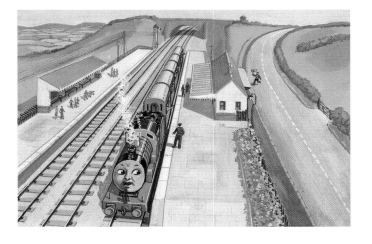

down the hill with his flags in one hand and a sandwich in the other.

He ran on to the platform, blew his whistle, and jumped into his van.

Edward puffed off. He did have a happy day. All the children ran to wave as he went past and he met old friends at all the stations. He worked so hard that the Driver promised to take him out again next day.

"I'm going out again tomorrow," he told the other engines that night in the shed. "What do you think of that?"

But he didn't hear what they thought, for he was so tired and happy that he fell asleep at once.

EDWARD AND GORDON

ILLUSTRATED BY C. REGINALD DALBY

ONE of the engines in Edward's shed was called Gordon. He was very big and very proud.

"You watch me this afternoon, little Edward," he boasted, "as I rush through with the express; that will be a splendid sight for you."

Just then his Driver pulled the lever. "Goodbye, little Edward," said Gordon, as he puffed away, "look out for me this afternoon!"

Edward went off, too, to do some shunting.

Edward liked shunting. It was fun playing with trucks. He would come up quietly and give them a pull.

"Oh! Oh! Oh! Oh! Oh!" screamed the trucks. "Whatever is happening?"

Then he would stop and the silly trucks would go bump into each other.

"Oh! Oh! Oh! Oh!" they cried again.

Edward pushed them until they were running nicely, and when they weren't expecting it he would stop; one of them would be sure to run on to another line. Edward played till there were no more trucks; then he stopped to rest.

Presently he heard a whistle. Gordon came puffing along, very slowly, and very crossly. Instead of nice shining coaches, he was pulling a lot of very dirty coal trucks.

"A goods train! A goods train! A goods train!" he grumbled. "The shame of it, the shame of it, the shame of it."

He went slowly through, with the trucks clattering and banging behind him.

Edward laughed, and went to find some more trucks.

Soon afterwards a porter came and spoke to his Driver. "Gordon can't get up the hill. Will you take Edward and push him, please?"

Edward's Driver came up. "We've come to push," he said. "No use at all," said Gordon. "You wait and see," said Edward's Driver.

They brought the train back to the bottom of the hill. Edward came up behind the brake van ready to push.

"Peep, peep, I'm ready," said Edward.

They found Gordon halfway up the hill and very cross. His Driver and Fireman were talking to him severely. "You are not trying!" they told him.

"I can't do it," said Gordon. "The noisy trucks hold an engine back so. If they were coaches now – clean sensible things that come quietly – that would be different."

"Poop, poop, no good," grumbled Gordon.

The Guard blew his whistle and they pulled and pushed as hard as they could.

"I can't do it, I can't do it, I can't do it," puffed Gordon.

"I will do it, I will do it, I will do it," puffed Edward.

"I can't do it, I will do it, I can't do it, I will do it, I can't do it, I will do it," they puffed together.

Edward pushed and puffed and puffed and pushed, as hard as ever he could, and almost before he realized it, Gordon found himself at the top of the hill.

"I've done it! I've done it! I've done it!" he said proudly, and forgot all about Edward pushing behind. He didn't wait to say "Thank you", but ran on

so fast that he passed two stations before his Driver could make him stop.

Edward had pushed so hard that when he got to the top he was out of breath.

Gordon ran on so fast that Edward was left behind.

The Guard waved and waved, but Edward couldn't catch up.

He ran on to the next station, and there the Driver and Fireman said they were very pleased with him. The Fireman gave him a nice long drink of water, and the Driver said, "I'll get out my paint tomorrow, and give you a beautiful new coat of blue with red stripes, then you'll be the smartest engine in the shed."

Cows!

ILLUSTRATED BY C. REGINALD DALBY

EDWARD the Blue Engine was getting old. His bearings were worn, and he clanked as he puffed along. He was taking twenty empty cattle trucks to a market-town.

The sun shone, the birds sang, and some cows grazed in a field by the line.

"Come on! Come on! Come on!" puffed Edward.

"Oh! Oh! Oh! Oh!" screamed the trucks.

Edward puffed and clanked; the trucks rattled and screamed. The cows were not used to trains; the noise and smoke disturbed them.

They twitched up their tails and ran.

They galloped across the field, broke through the fence, and charged the train between the thirteenth and fourteenth trucks. The coupling broke, and the last seven trucks left the rails. They were not damaged, and stayed upright. They ran for a short way along the sleepers before stopping.

Edward felt a jerk but didn't take much notice.

He was used to trucks.

"Bother those trucks!" he thought. "Why can't they come quietly?" He ran on to the next station before either he or his Driver realised what had happened.

When Gordon and Henry heard about the accident, they laughed and laughed. "Fancy allowing cows to break his train! They wouldn't dare do that to US. WE'd show them!" they boasted.

Edward pretended not to mind, but Toby was cross.

"You couldn't help it, Edward," he said. "They've never met cows. I have, and I know the trouble they are."

Some days later Gordon rushed through Edward's station.

"Poop poop!" he whistled, "mind the cows!"

"Haha, haha, haha!" he chortled, panting up the hill.

"Hurry, hurry, hurry!" puffed Gordon.

"Don't make such a fuss! Don't make such a fuss!" grumbled his coaches. They rumbled over the viaduct and roared through the next station.

A long straight stretch of line lay ahead. In the distance was a bridge. It had high parapets each side.

It seemed to Gordon that there was something on the bridge. His Driver thought so too. "Whoa, Gordon!" he said, and shut off steam.

"Pooh!" said Gordon, "it's only a cow!

"SHOOH! SHOOH!" he hissed, moving slowly on to the bridge.

But the cow wouldn't "Shooh"! She had lost her calf, and felt lonely. "Mooooh!" she said sadly, walking towards him.

Gordon stopped!

His Driver, Fireman and

some passengers tried to send her away, but she wouldn't go, so they gave it up.

Presently Henry arrived with a train from the other direction.

"What's this?" he said grandly. "A cow? I'll soon settle *her*. Be off! Be off!" he hissed; but the cow turned and "moohed" at him. Henry backed away. "I don't want to hurt her," he said.

Drivers, Firemen and passengers again tried to move the cow, but failed. Henry's Guard went back and put detonators on the line to protect his train. At

the nearest station he told them about the cow.

"That must be Bluebell," said a porter thoughtfully, "her calf is here, ready to go to market. We'll take it along."

So they unloaded the calf and took it to the bridge.

"Mooh! Mooh!" wailed the calf. "MOOH MOOH!" bellowed Bluebell.

She nuzzled her calf happily, and the porter led them away.

The two trains started.

"Not a word."

"Keep it dark," whispered Gordon and Henry as they passed; but the story soon spread.

"Well, well, well!" chuckled Edward, "two big engines afraid of one cow!"

"Afraid —— Rubbish," said Gordon huffily. "We didn't want the poor thing to hurt herself

by running against us. We stopped so as not to excite her. You see what I mean, my dear Edward."

"Yes, Gordon," said Edward gravely.

Gordon felt somehow that Edward "saw" only too well.

BERTIE'S CHASE

ILLUSTRATED BY C. REGINALD DALBY

"PEEP! Peep! We're late," fussed Edward. "Peep! Peeppipeep! Where is Thomas? He doesn't usually make us wait."

"Oh dear, what can the matter be? . . ." sang the Fireman, "Johnnie's so long at . . ."

"Never you mind about Johnnie," laughed the Driver, "just you climb on the cab, and look for Thomas."

"Can you see him?"

"No."

The Guard looked at his watch. "Ten minutes late!" he said to the Driver, "we can't wait here all day."

"Look again, Sid," said the Driver, "just in case."

The Fireman got to his feet.

"Can you see him?"

"No," he answered, "there's Bertie bus in a tearing hurry. No need to bother with him though; likely he's on a Coach Tour or something." He clambered down.

"Right away, Charlie," said

the Guard, and Edward puffed off.

"Toooot! TOOOOT! Stop! STOP!" wailed Bertie roaring into the Yard, but it was no good. Edward's last coach had disappeared into the tunnel.

"Bother!" said Bertie. "Bother Thomas' Fireman not coming to work today. Oh why did I promise to help the Passengers catch the train?"

"That will do, Bertie," said his Driver, "a promise is a promise and we must keep it."

"I'll catch Edward or bust," said Bertie grimly, as he raced along the road. "Oh my gears and axles!" he groaned, toiling up the hill. "I'll never be the same bus again!"

"Tootootoo Tootoot! I see him. Hurray! Hurray!" he cheered as he reached the top of the hill.

"He's reached the station," Bertie groaned the next minute.

"No . . . he's stopped by a signal. Hurray! Hurray!" and he tore down the hill, his brakes squealing at the corners.

His passengers bounced like balls in a bucket. "Well done, Bertie," they shouted. "Go it! Go it!"

Hens and dogs scattered in all directions as he raced through the village.

"Wait! Wait!" he tooted, skidding into the Yard.

He was just in time to see the signal drop, the Guard wave

his flag, and Edward puff out of the station.

His passengers rushed to the platform, but it was no good, and they came bustling back.

"I'm sorry," said Bertie unhappily.

"Never mind, Bertie," they said. "After him quickly. Third time lucky you know!"

"Do you think we'll catch him at the next station, Driver?"

"There's a good chance," he answered. "Our road keeps close to the line, and we can climb hills better than Edward."

He thought for a minute. "I'll just make sure." He then spoke to the Stationmaster, while the passengers waited impatiently in the bus.

"This hill is too steep! This hill is too steep!" grumbled the coaches as Edward snorted in front.

They reached the top at last and ran smoothly into the station.

"Peepeep!" whistled Edward, "get in quickly please."

The porters and people hurried and Edward impatiently waited to start.

"Peeeep!" whistled the Guard, and Edward's Driver looked back; but the flag didn't

wave. There was a distant "Tooootoooot!" and the Stationmaster, running across, snatched the green flag out of the Guard's hand.

Then everything seemed to happen at once.

"Too too TOOOOOOT!" bellowed Bertie; his passengers poured on to the platform and scrambled into the train. The Stationmaster told the Guard and Driver what had happened, and Edward listened.

"I'm sorry about the chase, Bertie," he said.

"My fault," panted Bertie, "late at junction. . . . You didn't know . . . about Thomas' passengers."

"Peepeep! Goodbye, Bertie, we're off!" whistled Edward.

"Three cheers for Bertie!" called the passengers. They cheered and waved till they were out of sight.

SAVED FROM SCRAP

ILLUSTRATED BY C. REGINALD DALBY

THERE is a scrap yard near Edward's station. It is full of rusty old cars and machinery. They are brought there to be broken up. The pieces are loaded

into trucks, and Edward pulls them to the Steelworks, where they are melted down and used again.

One day Edward saw a Traction-engine in the Yard.

"Hullo!" he said, "you're not broken and rusty. What are you doing there?"

"I'm Trevor," said the Traction-engine sadly, "they are

going to break me up next week."

"What a shame!" said Edward.

"My Driver says I only need some paint, Brasso, and oil, to be as good as new," Trevor went on sadly, "but it's no good, my Master doesn't want me. I suppose it's because I'm old-fashioned."

Edward snorted indignantly, "People say *I'm* old-fashioned, but I don't care. The Fat Controller says I'm a Useful Engine."

"My Driver says I'm useful too," replied Trevor. "I sometimes feel ill, but I don't give up like these tractors; I

struggle on and finish the job. I've never broken down in my life," he ended proudly.

"What work did you do?" asked Edward kindly.

"My Master would send us from farm to farm. We threshed the corn, hauled logs, sawed timber, and did lots of other work. We made friends at all the farms, and saw them every year. The children loved to see us come. They followed us in crowds, and watched us all day long. My Driver would sometimes give them rides."

Trevor shut his eyes —— remembering ——

"I like children," he said simply. "Oh yes, I like children."

"It's a shame! It's a shame!" he hissed as he brought his coaches to the station.

Then ——

"Peep! Peep!" he whistled, "why didn't I think of him before?"

Waiting there on the platform was the very person.

"'Morning Charlie, 'Morning Sid. Hullo Edward,

"Broken up, what a shame! Broken up, what a shame!" clanked Edward as he went back to work. "I *must* help Trevor, I *must*!"

He thought of the people he knew, who liked engines. Edward had lots of friends, but strangely none of them had room for a Traction-engine at home!

you look upset!"

"What's the matter, Charlie?" he asked the Driver.

"There's a Traction-engine in the scrap yard, Vicar; he'll be broken up next week, and it's a shame. Jem Cole says he never drove a better engine."

"Do save him, Sir! You've got room, Sir!"

"Yes, Edward, I've got room," laughed the Vicar, "but I don't need a Traction-engine!"

"He'll saw wood, and give children rides. Do buy him, Sir, please!"

"We'll see," said the Vicar, and climbed into the train.

Jem Cole came on Saturday afternoon. "The Reverend's coming to see you, Trevor; maybe he'll buy you."

"Do you think he will?" asked Trevor hopefully.

"He will when I've lit your fire, and cleaned you up," said Jem.

When the Vicar and his two boys arrived in the evening, Trevor was blowing off steam. He hadn't felt so happy for months.

"Watch this, Reverence," called Jem, and Trevor chuffered happily about the Yard.

"Oh Daddy, DO buy him," pleaded the boys, jumping up and down in their excitement.

"Now *I'll* try," and the Vicar climbed up beside Jem.

"Show your paces, Trevor," he said, and drove him about the Yard.

Then he went into the office, and came out smiling. "I've got him cheap, Jem, cheap."

"D'ye hear that, Trevor?" cried Jem. "The Reverend's saved you, and you'll live at the Vicarage now."

"Peep! Peep!" whistled Trevor happily.

"Will you drive him home for me, Jem, and take these scallywags with you? They won't want to come in the car when there's a Traction-engine to ride on!"

Trevor's home in the Vicarage Orchard is close to the railway, and he sees Edward every day. His paint is spotless and his brass shines like gold.

He saws firewood in winter, and Jem sometimes borrows him when a tractor fails. Trevor likes doing his old jobs, but his happiest day is the Church Fête. Then, with a long wooden seat bolted to his bunker, he chuffers round the Orchard giving rides to children.

Long afterwards you will see him shut his eyes —— remembering ——

"I like children," he whispers happily.

OLD IRON

ILLUSTRATED BY C. REGINALD DALBY

ONE day James had to wait at Edward's station till Edward and his train came in. This made him cross. "Late again!" he shouted.

Edward only laughed, and James fumed away.

"Edward is impossible," he grumbled to the others, "he clanks about like a lot of old iron, and he is so slow he makes us wait."

Thomas and Percy were indignant. "Old iron!" they snorted. "SLOW! Why! Edward could beat you in a race any day!"

"Really!" said James huffily, "I should like to see him do it."

One day James' Driver did not feel well when he came to work. "I'll manage," he said, but when they reached the top of Gordon's Hill, he could hardly stand.

The Fireman drove the train to the next station. He spoke to the Signalman, put the trucks in a siding, and uncoupled James ready for shunting.

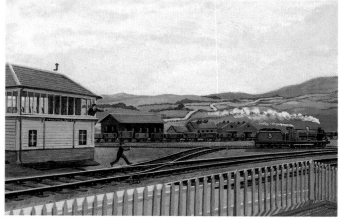

Then he helped the Driver over to the station, and asked them to look after him, and find a "Relief".

Suddenly the Signalman shouted, and the Fireman turned round and saw James puffing away.

He ran hard but he couldn't catch James, and soon came back to the signal box. The Signalman was busy. "All traffic halted," he announced at last. "Up and down main lines are clear for thirty miles, and the Inspector's coming."

The Fireman mopped his face. "What happened?" he asked.

"Two boys were on the footplate; they tumbled off when James started. I shouted at them and they ran like rabbits."

"Just let me catch them," said the Fireman grimly, "I'll teach them to meddle with my engine."

Both men jumped as the telephone rang; "Yes," answered the Signalman, "he's here . . . Right, I'll tell him.

"The Inspector's coming at once in Edward. He wants a shunter's pole, and a coil of wire rope."

"What for?" wondered the Fireman.

"Search me! But you'd better get them quickly."

The Fireman was ready and waiting when Edward arrived. The Inspector saw the pole and rope. "Good man," he said, "jump in."

"We'll catch him, we'll catch him," puffed Edward, crossing to the up line in pursuit.

James was laughing as he left the Yard. "What a lark! What a lark!" he chuckled to himself.

Presently he missed his Driver's hand on the regulator . . . and then he realised there was no one in his cab . . .

"What shall I do?" he wailed, "I can't stop. Help! Help!"

"We're coming, we're coming."

Edward was panting up behind with every ounce of steam he had. With a

great effort, he caught up, and crept alongside, slowly gaining till his smokebox was level with James' buffer-beam.

"Steady, Edward."

The Inspector stood on Edward's front, holding a noose of rope in the crook of the shunter's pole. He was trying to slip it over James' buffer. The engines swayed and lurched.

He tried again and again; more than once he nearly fell, but just saved himself.

At last – "Got him!" he shouted. He pulled the noose tight and came back to the cab safely.

Gently braking, so as not to snap the rope, Edward's Driver checked the engines' speed, and James' Fireman scrambled across and took control.

The engines puffed back side by side. "So the 'old iron' caught you after all!" chuckled Edward.

"I'm sorry," whispered James, "thank you for saving me."

"That's all right."

"You were splendid, Edward."

The Fat Controller was

waiting, and thanking the men warmly. "A fine piece of work," he said. "James, you can rest, and then take your train. I'm proud of you, Edward; you shall go to the Works, and have your worn parts mended."

"Oh! Thank you, Sir!" said Edward happily. "It'll be *lovely* not to clank."

The two naughty boys were soon caught by the police, and their fathers walloped them soundly.

They were also forbidden to watch trains till they could be trusted.

James' Driver soon got well in hospital, and is now back at work. James missed him very much, but he missed Edward more, and you will be glad to know that, when Edward came home the other day, James and all the other engines gave him a tremendous welcome.

The Fat Controller thinks he will be deaf for weeks!

EDWARD'S EXPLOIT

ILLUSTRATED BY GUNVOR AND PETER EDWARDS

EDWARD scolded the twins severely, but told Gordon it served him right. Gordon was furious.

A few days later, some Enthusiasts came. On their last afternoon they went to the China Clay Works.

Edward found it hard to start the heavy train.

"Did you see him straining?" asked Henry.

"Positively painful," remarked James.

"Just pathetic," grunted Gordon. "He should give up and be Preserved before it's too late."

"Shut up!" burst out Duck. "You're all jealous. Edward's better than any of you."

"You're right, Duck," said BoCo. "Edward's old, but he'll surprise us all."

Bill and Ben were delighted with their visitors. They loved being photographed and took the party to the Workings in a "Brake Van Special".

On the way home, however, the weather changed. Wind and rain buffeted Edward. His sanding gear failed, his wheels slipped, and his Fireman rode in front dropping sand on the rails by hand.

"ComeOn-ComeOn-ComeOn," panted Edward breathlessly. "This is dreadful!"

But there was worse to come. Before his Driver could check them, his wheels slipped fiercely again and again.

With a shrieking crack, something broke and battered his frame and splashers up and out of shape.

The passengers gathered round while the crew inspected the damage. Repairs took some time.

"One of your crank-pins broke, Edward," said his Driver at last. "We've taken your side-rods off. Now you're a 'single' like an old fashioned engine. Can you get these people home? They must start back tonight."

"I'll try, Sir," promised Edward.

They backed down to where the line was more nearly level. Edward puffed and pulled his hardest, but his wheels kept slipping and he just could not start the heavy train.

The passengers were getting anxious.

Driver, Fireman and Guard went along the train making adjustments between the coaches.

"We've loosened the couplings, Edward," they said. "Now you can pick your coaches up one by one, just as you do with trucks."

"That will be much easier," said Edward gratefully.

So, with the Fireman sanding carefully in front, the Driver gently opened the regulator.

Come . . . on! puffed Edward. He moved cautiously forward, ready to take the strain as his tender coupling tightened against the weight of the first coach.

The first coach moving, helped to start the second, the second helped the third, and so on down the train.

"I've done it! I've done it!" puffed Edward, his wheels spinning with excitement.

"Steady, Boy!" warned his Driver, skilfully checking the wheel-slip. "Well done, Boy!"

"You've got them! You've *got* them!" And he listened happily to Edward's steady beat as he forged slowly but surely up the hill.

The passengers were thrilled. Most had their heads out of windows. They waved and shouted, cheering Edward on.

The Fat Controller paced the platform. Henry with the Special train waited anxiously too.

They heard a "Peep peep!" Then, battered, weary, but unbeaten, Edward steamed in.

The Fat Controller stepped angrily forward. He pointed to the clock, but excited passengers swept him aside. They cheered Edward, his Driver and Fireman to the echo, before rushing off to get in Henry's train.

Henry steamed away to another storm of cheers, but not before everyone knew Edward's story.

Edward went thankfully to the Shed, while Duck and BoCo saw to it that he was left in peace. Gordon and James remained respectfully silent.

The Fat Controller asked BoCo to look after Edward's line while he was being mended. BoCo was pleased. He worked well, and now they run it together. Bill and Ben still tease him, but BoCo doesn't mind.

He lives at Edward's station, but is welcome anywhere, for he is now one of the "family".

Donald and Douglas were the last to accept him, but he often helps with their goods trains, and the other day they were heard to remark, "For a diesel, yon BoCo's nae sich a bad sort of engine."

That, from the Caledonian Twins, is high praise indeed!

GORDON
the Big Engine

In which Gordon falls into a ditch,

travels to London and finally

makes friends with Thomas . . .

OFF THE RAILS

ILLUSTRATED BY C. REGINALD DALBY

GORDON was resting in a siding.

"Peep peep! Peep peep! Hullo, Fatface!" whistled Henry.

"What cheek!" spluttered Gordon. "That Henry is too big for his wheels; fancy speaking to me like that! Me e e e e!" he went on, letting off steam, "Me e e e who has never had an accident!"

"Aren't jammed whistles and burst safety valves accidents?" asked Percy innocently.

"No indeed!" said Gordon huffily, "high spirits – might happen to any engine; but to come off the rails, well I ask you! Is it right? Is it decent?"

A few days later it was Henry's turn to take the Express. Gordon watched him getting ready.

"Be careful, Henry," he said, "You're not pulling the 'Flying Kipper' now; mind you keep on the rails today."

Henry snorted away, Gordon yawned and went to sleep.

But he didn't sleep long. "Wake up, Gordon," said his Driver, "a Special train's coming and we're to pull it."

Gordon opened his eyes. "Is it Coaches or Trucks?"

"Trucks," said his Driver.

"Trucks!" said Gordon crossly. "Pah!"

They lit Gordon's fire and oiled him ready for the run. The fire was sulky and wouldn't burn; but they couldn't wait, so Edward pushed him to the turntable to get him facing the right way.

"I *won't* go, I *won't* go," grumbled Gordon.

"Don't be silly, don't be silly," puffed Edward.

Gordon tried hard, but he couldn't stop himself being moved.

At last he was on the turntable, Edward was uncoupled and backed away, and Gordon's Driver and Fireman jumped down to turn him round.

The movement had shaken Gordon's fire; it was now burning nicely and making steam.

Gordon was cross, and didn't care what he did.

He waited till the table was half-way round. "I'll show them! I'll show them!" he hissed, and moved slowly forward.

He only meant to go a little way, just far enough to "jam" the table, and stop it turning, as he had done once before. But he couldn't stop himself, and, slithering down the embankment, he settled in a ditch.

"Oooosh!" he hissed as his wheels churned the mud. "Get me out! Get me out!"

"Not a hope," said his Driver and Fireman, "you're stuck, you silly great engine, don't you understand that?"

They telephoned the Fat Controller.

"So Gordon didn't want to take the Special and ran into a ditch," he answered from his office. "What's that you say? The Special's waiting – tell Edward to take it please – and Gordon? Oh leave him where he is; we haven't time to bother with him now."

A family of toads croaked crossly at Gordon as he lay in the mud. On the other side of the ditch some little boys were chattering.

"Coo! Doesn't he look silly!"

"They'll never get him out."

They began to sing:

Silly old Gordon fell in a ditch,
fell in a ditch,
fell in a ditch,
Silly old Gordon fell in a ditch,
All on a Monday morning.

The School bell rang and, still singing, they chased down the road.

"Pshaw!" said Gordon, and blew away three tadpoles and an inquisitive newt.

Gordon lay in the ditch all day.

"Oh dear!" he thought, "I shall never get out."

But that evening they brought floodlights; then with powerful jacks they lifted Gordon and made a road of sleepers under his wheels to keep him from the mud.

Strong wire ropes were fastened to his back end, and James and Henry, pulling hard, at last managed to bring him to the rails.

Late that night Gordon crawled home a sadder and a wiser engine!

LEAVES

ILLUSTRATED BY C. REGINALD DALBY

Two men were cleaning Gordon.

"Mind my eye," Gordon grumbled.

"Shut it, silly! Did ever you see such mud, Bert?"

"No I never, Alf! You ought to be ashamed, Gordon, giving us extra work."

The hosing and scrubbing stopped. Gordon opened one eye, but shut it quickly.

"Wake up, Gordon," said the Fat Controller sternly, "and listen to me. You will pull no more coaches till you are a Really Useful Engine."

So Gordon had to spend his time pulling trucks.

"Goods trains, Goods trains," he muttered. He felt his position deeply.

"That's for you! – and *you!* – *and* you!" Gordon said crossly.

"Oh! Oh! Oh! Oh!" screamed the trucks as he shunted them about the Yard.

"Trucks will be trucks," said James, watching him.

"They won't with *me!*" snorted Gordon. "I'll teach them. Go on!" and another truck scurried away.

"They tried to push me down the hill this morning," Gordon explained. "It's slippery there. You'll probably need some help."

"*I* don't need help on hills," said James huffily.

Gordon laughed, and got ready for his next train.

James went away to take the Express.

"Slippery hills indeed," he snorted. "*I* don't need help."

"Come on! Come on!" he puffed.

"All in good time, all in good time," grumbled the coaches.

The train was soon running nicely, but a "Distant" signal checked them close to Gordon's Hill.

Gordon's Hill used to be bleak and bare. Strong winds from the sea made it hard to climb. Trees were planted to give shelter, and in summer the trains run through a leafy avenue.

Now autumn had come, and dead leaves fell. The wind usually puffed them away, but today rain made them heavy, and they did not move.

The "Home" signal showed "clear", and James began to go faster.

He started to climb the hill.

"I'll do it! I'll do it!" he puffed confidently.

Half-way up he was not so sure! "I *must* do it, I *must* do it," he panted desperately, but try as he would, his wheels slipped on the leaves, and he couldn't pull the train at all.

"Whatsthematter? Whatsthematter?" he gasped.

"Steady old boy, steady," soothed his Driver.

His Fireman put sand on the rails to help him grip; but James' wheels spun so fast that they only ground the sand and leaves to slippery mud, making things worse than before.

The train slowly stopped. Then –

"Help! Help! Help!" whistled James; for though his wheels were turning forwards, the heavy coaches pulled him backwards, and the whole train started slipping down the hill.

His Driver shut off steam, carefully put on the brakes, and skillfully stopped the train.

"Whew!" he sat down and mopped his face. "I've never known *that* happen before."

"I have," said the Fireman, "in Bincombe tunnel – Southern Region."

The Guard poked his head in the cab. "Now what?" he asked.

"Back to the station," said the Fireman, taking charge, "and send for a 'Banker'."

So the Guard warned the

Signalman, and they brought the train safely down.

But Gordon, who had followed with a goods train, saw what had happened.

Gordon left his trucks, and crossed over to James.

"I thought you could climb hills," he chuckled.

James didn't answer; he had no steam!

"Ah well! We live and learn," said Gordon, "we live and learn. Never mind, little James," he went on kindly, "I'm

going to push behind. Whistle when you're ready."

James waited till he had plenty of steam, then "Peep! Peep!" he called.

"Poop! Poop! Poop!"

"Pull hard," puffed Gordon.

"We'll do it!" puffed James.

"Pull hard! We'll do it," the engines puffed together.

Clouds of smoke and steam towered from the snorting engines as they struggled up the hill.

"We *can* do it!" puffed James.

"We *will* do it!" puffed Gordon.

The greasy rails sometimes made Gordon's wheels slip, but he never gave up, and presently they reached the top.

"We've done it! We've done it!" they puffed.

Gordon stopped. "Poop! Poop! He whistled. "Goodbye."

"Peep! Peep! Peep! Peep! Thank you! Goodbye," answered James. Gordon watched the coaches wistfully till they were out of sight; then slowly he trundled back to his waiting trucks.

DOWN THE MINE

ILLUSTRATED BY C. REGINALD DALBY

ONE day Thomas was at the junction, when Gordon shuffled in with some trucks.

"Poof!" remarked Thomas, "what a funny smell!"

"Can you smell a smell?"

"I can't smell a smell," said Annie and Clarabel.

"A funny, musty sort of smell," said Thomas.

"No one noticed it till you did," grunted Gordon. "It must be yours."

"Annie! Clarabel! Do you know what I think it is?" whispered Thomas loudly. "It's ditchwater!"

Gordon snorted, but before he could answer, Thomas puffed quickly away.

Annie and Clarabel could hardly believe their ears!

"He's *dreadfully* rude; I feel quite ashamed." "I feel *quite* ashamed, he's dreadfully rude," they twittered to each other.

"You mustn't be rude, you make us ashamed," they kept telling Thomas.

But Thomas didn't care a bit.

"That was funny, that was funny," he chuckled. He felt very pleased with himself.

Annie and Clarabel were deeply shocked. They had a great respect for Gordon the Big Engine.

Thomas left the coaches at a station and went to a mine for some trucks.

Long ago, miners, digging for lead, had made tunnels under the ground.

Though strong enough to hold up trucks, their roofs could not bear the weight of engines.

A large notice said: "DANGER, ENGINES MUST NOT PASS THIS BOARD."

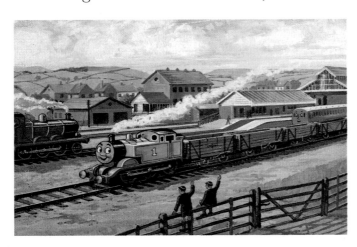

Thomas had often been warned, but he didn't care.

"Silly old board," he thought. He had often tried to pass it, but had never succeeded.

This morning he laughed as he puffed along. He had made a plan.

He had to push empty trucks into one siding, and pull out full ones from another.

His Driver stopped him, and the Fireman went to turn the points.

"Come on," waved the Fireman, and they started.

The Driver leaned out of the cab to see where they were going.

"Now!" said Thomas to himself, and, bumping the trucks fiercely, he jerked his Driver off the footplate.

"Hurrah!" laughed Thomas, and he followed the trucks into the siding.

"Stupid old board!" said Thomas as he passed it. "There's no danger; there's no danger."

His Driver, unhurt, jumped up. "Look out!" he shouted.

The Fireman clambered into the cab. Thomas squealed crossly as his brakes were applied.

"It's quite safe," he hissed.

"Come back," yelled the Driver, but before they could move, there was rumbling and the rails quivered.

The Fireman jumped clear. As he did so the ballast slipped away and the rails sagged and broke.

"Fire and Smoke!" said Thomas, "I'm sunk!" – and he was!

Thomas could just see out of the hole, but he couldn't move.

"Oh dear!" he said, "I am a silly engine."

"And a very naughty one too," said a voice behind him, "I saw you."

"Please get me out; I won't be naughty again."

"I'm not so sure," replied the Fat Controller. "We can't lift you out with a crane, the ground's not firm enough. Hm . . . Let me see . . . I wonder if Gordon could pull you out."

"Yes Sir," said Thomas nervously. He didn't want to meet Gordon just yet!

"Down a mine is he? Ho! Ho! Ho!" laughed Gordon.

"What a joke! What a joke!" he chortled, puffing to the rescue.

"Poop! Poop! Little Thomas," he whistled, "we'll have you out in a couple of puffs."

Strong cables were fastened between the two engines.

"Poop! Poop! Poop!"

"Are you ready? HEAVE," called the Fat Controller.

But they didn't pull Thomas out in two puffs; Gordon was panting hard and nearly purple before he had dragged Thomas out of the hold, and safely past the board.

"I'm sorry I was cheeky," said Thomas.

"That's all right, Thomas. You made me laugh. I like that. I'm in

disgrace," Gordon went on pathetically, "I feel very low."

"I'm in disgrace too," said Thomas.

"Why! so you are Thomas; we're both in disgrace. Shall we form an Alliance?"

"An Ally – what – was – it?"

"An Alliance, Thomas, 'United we stand, together we fall'," said Gordon grandly.

"You help me, and I help you. How about it?"

"Right you are," said Thomas.

"Good! That's settled," rumbled Gordon.

And buffer to buffer the Allies puffed home.

PAINT POTS AND QUEENS

ILLUSTRATED BY C. REGINALD DALBY

THE stations on the line were being painted.

The engines were surprised.

"The Queen is coming," said the painters. The engines in their Shed were excited and wondered who would pull the Royal Train.

"I'm too old to pull important trains," said Edward sadly.

"I'm in disgrace," Gordon said gloomily. "The Fat Controller would never choose me."

"He'll choose me, of course," boasted James the Red Engine.

"You!" Henry snorted, "*You* can't climb hills. He will ask *me* to pull it, *and* I'll have a new coat of paint. You wait and see."

The days passed. Henry puffed about proudly, quite sure that he would be the Royal Engine.

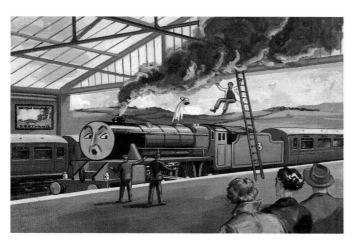

One day when it rained, his Driver and Fireman stretched a tarpaulin from the cab to the tender, to keep themselves dry.

Henry puffed into the Big Station. A painter was climbing a ladder above the line. Henry's smoke puffed upwards; it was thick and black. The painter choked and couldn't see. He missed his footing on the ladder, dropped his paint pot, and fell plop on to Henry's tarpaulin.

The paint poured over Henry's boiler, and trickled down each side. The paint pot perched on his dome.

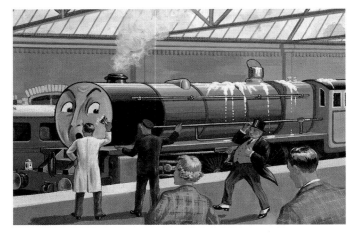

The painter clambered down and shook his brush at Henry.

"You spoil my clean paint with your dirty smoke," he said, "and then you take the whole lot, and make me go and fetch some more." He stumped crossly away.

The Fat Controller pushed through the crowd.

"You look like an iced cake, Henry," he said. "*That* won't do for the Royal Train. I must make other arrangements."

He walked over to the Yard.

Gordon and Thomas saw him coming, and both began to speak.

"Please Sir ———"

"One at a time," smiled the Fat Controller. "Yes Gordon?"

"May Thomas have his Branch Line again?"

"Hm," said the Fat Controller, "well Thomas?"

"Please, Sir, can Gordon pull coaches now?"

The Fat Controller pondered.

"Hm —— you've both been quite good lately, and you deserve a treat —— When the Queen comes, Edward will go in front and clear the line, Thomas will look after the coaches, and Gordon —— will pull the train."

"Ooooh Sir!" said the engines happily.

The great day came. Percy, Toby, Henry and James worked hard bringing people to the town.

Thomas sorted all their coaches in the Yard.

"Peep! Peep! Peep! They're coming!" Edward steamed in, looking smart with flags and bright paint.

Two minutes passed – five – seven – ten. "Poop! Poop!" Everyone knew that whistle, and a mighty cheer went up as the Queen's train glided into the station.

Gordon was spotless, and his brass shone. Like Edward, he was decorated with flags, but on his buffer beam he proudly carried the Royal Arms.

The Queen was met by the Fat Controller, and before doing anything else, she thanked him for their splendid run.

"Not at all, Your Majesty," he said, "thank *you*."

"We have read," said the Queen to the Fat Controller, "a great deal about your engines. May we see them please?"

So he led the way to where all the engines were waiting.

"Peep! Peep!" whistled Toby and Percy, "they're coming!"

"Sh Sh! Sh Sh!" hissed Henry and James.

But Toby and Percy were too excited to care.

The Fat Controller told the Queen their names, and she talked to each engine. Then she turned to go.

Percy bubbled over, "Three cheers for the Queen!" he called.

"Peeeep! Peeeep! Peeeep!" whistled all the engines.

The Fat Controller held his ears, but the Queen, smiling, waved to the engines till she passed the gate.

Next day the Queen spoke specially to Thomas, who fetched her coaches,

and to Edward and Gordon who took her away; and no engines ever felt prouder than Thomas, and Edward, and Gordon the Big Engine.

GORDON GOES FOREIGN

ILLUSTRATED BY JOHN T. KENNEY

LOTS of people travel to the Big Station at the end of the line. Engines from the Other Railway sometimes pull their trains. These engines stay the night and go home next day.

Gordon was talking one day to one of these.

"When I was young and green," he said, "I remember going to London. Do you know the place? The station's called King's Cross."

"King's Cross!" snorted the engine, "London's Euston. Everybody knows that."

"Rubbish!" said Duck, "London's Paddington. I *know*. I worked there."

They argued till they went to sleep. They argued when they woke up. They were still arguing when the other engine went away.

"Stupid thing," said Gordon crossly, "I've no patience."

"Stupid yourself," said Duck, "London's Paddington, PADDINGTON, do you hear?"

"Stop arguing," James broke in, "you make me tired. You're both agreed about something anyway."

"What's that?"

"London's not Euston," laughed James. "Now shut up!"

Gordon rolled away still grumbling. "I'm sure it's King's Cross. I'll go and prove it."

But that was easier said than done.

London lay beyond the Big Station at the other end of the Line. Gordon had to stop there. Another engine then took his train.

"If I didn't stop," he thought, "I could go to London."

One day he ran right through the station. Another time he tried to start before the Fireman could uncouple the coaches. He tried all sorts of tricks; but it was no good. His Driver checked him every time.

"Oh dear!" he thought sadly, "I'll never get there."

One day he pulled the Express to the station as usual. His Fireman uncoupled the coaches, and he ran on to his siding to wait till it was time to go home.

The coaches waited and waited at the platform; but their engine didn't come.

A porter ran across and spoke to Gordon's Driver. "The Inspector's on the platform. He wants to see you."

The Driver climbed down from the cab and walked over the station. He came back in a few minutes looking excited.

"Hullo!" said the Fireman, "what's happened?"

"The engine for the Express turned over when it was coming out of the Yard. Nothing else can come in or out. They want us to take the train to London. I said we would, if the Fat Controller agreed. They telephoned, and he said we could do it. How's that?"

"Fine," said the Fireman, "we'll show them what the Fat Controller's

engines can do."

"Come on!" said Gordon, "let's go." He rolled quickly over the crossings and backed on to the train.

It was only a few minutes before the Guard blew his whistle; but Gordon thought it was ages!

"COME ON! COME ON!" he puffed to the coaches.

"Comeoncomeoncomeon!"

"We're going to Town, we're going to Town," sang the coaches slowly at first, then faster and faster.

Gordon found that London was a long way away. "Never mind," he said, "I like a good long run to stretch my wheels."

But all the same he was glad when London came in sight.

The Fat Controller came into his office next morning. He looked at the letters on his desk. One had a London post-mark.

"I wonder how Gordon's getting on," he said.

The Stationmaster knocked and came in. He looked excited.

"Excuse me Sir, have you seen the news?"

"Not yet. Why?"

"Just look at this Sir."

The Fat Controller took the

Newspaper. "Good gracious me!" he said, "there's Gordon. Headlines too! 'FAMOUS ENGINE AT LONDON STATION. POLICE CALLED TO CONTROL CROWDS.'"

The Fat Controller read on, absorbed.

Gordon returned next day. The Fat Controller spoke to his Driver and Fireman. "I see you had a good welcome in London."

"We certainly did Sir! We signed autographs till our arms ached, and Gordon had his photograph taken from so many directions at once that he didn't know which way to look!"

"Good!" smiled the Fat Controller, "I expect he enjoyed himself. Didn't you Gordon?"

"No Sir, I didn't."

"Why ever not?"

"London's all wrong," answered Gordon sadly, "they've changed it. It isn't King's Cross any more. It's St Pancras."

DOMELESS ENGINES

ILLUSTRATED BY JOHN T. KENNEY

A SPECIAL train arrived one day, and the Fat Controller welcomed the passengers. They looked at everything in the Yard, and photographed the

engines. Duck's Driver let some of them ride in his cab.

"They're the Railway Society," his Driver explained. "They've come to see us. Their engine's 'City of Truro'. He was the first to go 100 miles an hour. Let's get finished, then we can go and talk to him."

"Oh!" said Duck, awed. "He's too famous to notice me."

"Rubbish!" smiled his Driver. "Come on."

Duck found "City of Truro" at the coaling stage.

"May I talk to you?" he asked shyly.

"Of course," smiled the famous engine, "I see you are one of Us."

"I try to teach them Our ways," said Duck modestly.

"All ship-shape and Swindon fashion. That's right."

"Please, could you tell me how you beat the South Western?"

So "City of Truro" told Duck all about his famous run from Plymouth to Bristol more than fifty years ago. They were

soon firm friends, and talked "Great Western" till late at night.

"City of Truro" left early next morning.

"Good riddance!" grumbled Gordon. "Chattering all night keeping important engines awake! Who *is* he anyway?"

"He's 'City of Truro'. He's famous."

"As famous as me? Nonsense!"

"He's famouser than you. He went 100 miles an hour before you were drawn or thought of."

"So he says; but I didn't like his looks. *He's got no dome*," said Gordon darkly. "Never trust domeless engines, they're not respectable.

"I never boast," Gordon continued modestly; "but 100 miles an hour would be easy for me. Goodbye!"

Presently Duck took some trucks to Edward's station. He was cross, and it was lucky for those trucks that they tried no tricks.

"Hullo!" called Edward. "The famous 'City of Truro' came though this morning. He whistled to me; wasn't he kind?"

"He's the finest engine in the world," said Duck, and he told Edward about "City of Truro", and what Gordon had said.

"Don't take any notice," soothed Edward, "he's just jealous. He thinks no engine should be famous but him. Look! He's coming now."

Gordon's boiler seemed to have swollen larger than ever. He was running very fast. He swayed up and down and from side to side as his wheels pounded the rails.

"He did it! I'll do it! He did it! I'll do it!" he panted. His train rocketed past and was gone.

Edward chuckled and winked at Duck. "Gordon's trying to do a 'City of Truro'," he said.

Duck was still cross. "I should think he'll knock himself to bits," he snorted. "I heard something rattle as he went through."

Gordon's Driver eased him off. "Steady boy!" he said. "We aren't running a race."

"We are then," said Gordon; but he said it to himself.

"I've never known him ride so roughly before," remarked his Driver.

His Fireman grabbed the brake handle to steady himself. "He's giving himself a hammering, and no mistake."

Soon Gordon began to feel a little queer. "The top of my boiler seems funny," he thought; "it's just as if something was loose. I'd better

go slower."

But by then it was too late!

They met the wind on the viaduct. It wasn't just a gentle wind; nor was it a hard steady wind. It was a teasing wind which blew suddenly in hard puffs, and caught you unawares.

Gordon thought it wanted to push him off the bridge. "No you don't!" he said firmly.

But the wind had other ideas. It curled round his boiler, crept under his loose dome, and lifted it off and away into the valley below. It fell on the rocks with a clang.

Gordon was most uncomfortable. He felt cold where his dome wasn't, and besides, people laughed at him as he passed.

At the Big Station, he tried to "Wheeeesh" them away; but they crowded round no matter what he did.

On the way back, he wanted his Driver to stop and find his dome, and was very cross when he wouldn't.

He hoped the Shed would be empty; but all the engines were there waiting.

"Never trust domeless engines," said a voice. "They aren't respectable."

WRONG ROAD

ILLUSTRATED BY GUNVOR AND PETER EDWARDS

THOMAS' Branch Line is important, and so is Edward's. They both bring in valuable traffic, but their track and bridges are not so strong as those on the Main.

That is why the Fat Controller does not allow the heavier Main Line Engines such as Gordon and Henry to run on them.

If, however, you had heard Gordon talking to Edward a short while ago, you would have thought that the Fat Controller had forbidden him to run on Branch Lines for quite another reason.

"It's not fair," grumbled Gordon.

"What isn't fair?" asked Edward.

"Letting Branch Line diesels pull Main Line trains."

"Never mind, Gordon. I'm sure BoCo will let you pull his trucks sometimes. That would make it quite fair."

Gordon spluttered furiously. "I *won't* pull BoCo's dirty trucks. I *won't* run on Branch Lines."

"Why not? It would be a nice change."

"The Fat Controller would never approve," said Gordon loftily. "Branch Lines are vulgar."

He puffed away in a dignified manner. Edward chuckled and followed him to the station . . .

Gordon, his Driver and his Fireman all say it was the lady's fault. She wore a green floppy hat, and was saying "Goodbye" to a friend sitting in the coach nearest the Guard's Van.

It was almost time to start. The Fireman looked back. He was new to the job. He couldn't see the Guard but he did see something green waving. He thought it was the flag.

"Right away, Mate," he called.

But the Guard had not waved his flag. When Gordon started he left some luggage, several indignant passengers and the Guard all standing on the platform.

Every evening two fast trains leave the Big Station within five minutes. The 6.25 is Gordon's for the Main Line. Edward's, at 6.30, runs along the Branch.

By the time Gordon had been brought back, Edward's train was overdue.

"You've missed your 'path', Gordon," said the Fat Controller, crossly. "Now we must clear Edward's train before you can start."

This should have put everything right with the least possible trouble; but Control at the Big Station made things worse. They forgot to warn the Signalman at Edward's Junction about the change of plan.

It was dark by the time the trains reached the junction, and you can guess what happened – Edward went through on the Main, while Gordon was switched to the Branch . . .

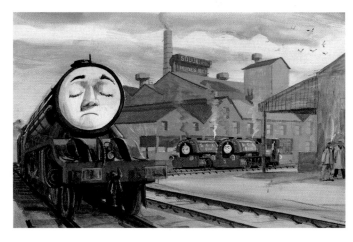

It took the Fat Controller several hours to sort out the tangle and pacify the passengers.

In the end Gordon was left, with his fire drawn, cold and cross on one of Edward's sidings.

Bill and Ben peeped into the Yard next morning. They wondered if BoCo had brought them some trucks. There were no trucks, but they didn't mind that.

Teasing Gordon, they thought, would be much better fun!

"What's that?" asked Bill loudly.

"Ssh!" whispered Ben. "It's Gordon."

"It *looks* like Gordon, but it can't be. Gordon *never* comes on Branch Lines. He thinks them vulgar."

Gordon pretended he hadn't heard.

"If it isn't Gordon," said Ben, "it's just a pile of old iron . . . "

". . . which we'd better take to the scrapyard."

"No, Bill, this lot's useless for scrap. We'll take it to the harbour and dump it in the sea."

Gordon was alarmed. "I *am* Gordon. Stop! Stop!"

The twins paid no attention. Gordon shut his eyes and prepared for the worst.

The twins argued loudly and long. Bill favoured the

scrapyard, while Ben said that the cutting up in such places was something cruel.

It would be kinder, he urged, to give these remains a quick end in the sea.

Besides, he went on, they would make a lovely splash.

Gordon could not view either prospect with any enthusiasm.

Up to that time he had disapproved of diesels.

They were, he considered, ugly, smelly, and noisy; but when he opened his eyes and saw BoCo coming into the

Yard, he thought him the most beautiful sight he had ever seen.

"BoCo my dear engine!" he gasped. "Save me!"

BoCo quickly sized up the situation, and sent Bill and Ben about their business.

They were cheeky at first, but BoCo threatened to take away the trucks of coal he had brought for them. That made them behave at once.

Gordon thought he was wonderful. "Those little demons!" he said. "How do you do it?"

"Ah well," said BoCo. "It's just a knack."

Gordon thinks to this day that BoCo saved his life; but we know that the twins were only teasing – don't we?

HENRY
the Green Engine

In which Henry becomes ill,

gets well again and then becomes

a brand-new engine . . .

The Sad Story of Henry

ILLUSTRATED BY C. REGINALD DALBY

Once, an engine attached
to a train
Was afraid of a few drops
of rain —
— It went into a tunnel,
And squeaked through
its funnel
And never came out again.

The engine's name was Henry. His Driver and Fireman argued with him, but he would not move. "The rain will spoil my lovely green paint and red stripes," he said.

The Guard blew his whistle till he had no more breath, and waved his flags till his arms ached; but Henry still stayed in the tunnel, and blew steam at him.

"I am not going to spoil my

lovely green paint and red stripes for you," he said rudely.

The passengers came and argued too, but Henry would not move.

A Fat Director who was on the train told the Guard to get a rope. "We will pull you out," he said. But Henry only blew steam at him and made him wet.

They hooked the rope on and all pulled – except the Fat Director. "My doctor has forbidden me to pull," he said.

They pulled and pulled and pulled, but still Henry stayed in the tunnel.

Then they tried pushing from the other end. The Fat Director said, "One, two, three, push": but did not help. "My doctor has forbidden me to push," he said.

They pushed and pushed and pushed; but still Henry stayed in the tunnel.

At last another train came. The Guard waved his red flag and stopped it. The two engine Drivers, the two Firemen, and the two Guards went and argued with Henry. "Look, it has stopped raining," they said. "Yes, but it will begin again

soon," said Henry. "And what would become of my green paint with red stripes then?"

So they brought the other engine up, and it pushed and puffed, and puffed and pushed as hard as ever it could. But still Henry stayed in the tunnel.

So they gave it up. They told Henry, "We shall leave you there for always and always and always."

They took up the old rails, built a wall in front of him, and cut a new tunnel.

Now Henry can't get out, and he watches the trains rushing through the new tunnel. He is very sad because no one will ever see his lovely green paint with red stripes again.

But I think he deserved it, don't you?

Edward, Gordon and Henry

ILLUSTRATED BY C. REGINALD DALBY

Edward and Gordon often went through the tunnel where Henry was shut up.

Edward would say, "Peep, peep – hullo!" and Gordon would say, "Poop, poop, poop! Serves you right!"

Poor Henry had no steam to answer, his fire had gone out; soot and dirt from the tunnel roof had spoilt his lovely green paint and red stripes. He was cold and unhappy, and wanted to come out and pull trains too.

Gordon always pulled the Express. He was proud of being the only engine strong enough to do it.

There were many heavy coaches, full of important people like the Fat Director who had punished Henry.

Gordon was seeing how fast he could go. "Hurry! Hurry! Hurry!" he panted.

"Trickety-trock, trickety-trock, trickety-trock," said the coaches.

Gordon could see Henry's tunnel in front.

"In a minute," he thought, "I'll poop, poop, poop at Henry, and rush through and out into the open again."

Closer and closer he came – he was almost there, when crack: "Wheee ———— eeshshsh," he was in a cloud of steam, and going slower and slower.

His Driver stopped the train.

"What has happened to me?" asked Gordon, "I feel so weak." "You've burst your safety valve," said the Driver. "You can't pull the train any more." "Oh, dear," said Gordon. "We were going so nicely, too. . . . Look at Henry laughing at me." Gordon made a face at Henry, and blew smoke at him.

Everybody got out, and came to see Gordon. "Humph!" said the Fat Director. "I never liked these big engines – always going wrong; send for another engine at once."

While the Guard went to find one, they uncoupled Gordon, and ran him on a siding out of the way.

The only engine left in the Shed was Edward.

"I'll come and try," he said.

Gordon saw him coming. "That's no use," he said, "Edward can't pull the train."

Edward puffed and pulled, and pulled and puffed, but he couldn't move the heavy coaches.

"I told you so," said Gordon rudely. "Why not let Henry try?"

"Yes," said the Fat Director, "I will."

"Will you help pull this train, Henry?" he asked. "Yes," said Henry at once.

So Gordon's Driver and Fireman lit his fire; some platelayers broke down the wall and put back the rails; and when he had steam up Henry puffed out.

He was dirty, his boiler was black, and he was covered with cobwebs. "Ooh! I'm so stiff! Ooh! I'm so stiff!" he groaned.

"You'd better have a run to ease your joints, and find a turntable," said the Fat Director kindly.

Henry came back feeling better, and they put him in front.

"Peep, peep," said Edward, "I'm ready."

"Peep, peep, peep," said Henry, "so am I."

"Pull hard; pull hard; pull hard," puffed Edward.

"We'll do it; we'll do it; we'll do it," puffed Henry.

"Pull hard we'll do it. Pull hard we'll do it. Pull hard we'll do it," they puffed together. The

heavy coaches jerked and began to move, slowly at first, then faster and faster.

"We've done it together! We've done it together! We've done it together!" said Edward and Henry.

"You've done it, hurray! You've done it, hurray! You've done it, hurray!" sang the coaches.

All the passengers were excited. The Fat Director leaned out of the window to wave to Edward and Henry; but the train was going so fast that his hat blew off into a field where a goat ate it for his tea.

They never stopped till they came to the big station at the end of the line.

The passengers all got out and said, "Thank you," and the Fat Director promised Henry a new coat of paint.

"Would you like blue and red?"

"Yes, please," said Henry, "then I'll be like Edward."

Edward and Henry went home quietly, and on their way they helped Gordon back to the shed.

All three engines are now great friends.

Wasn't Henry pleased when he had his new coat. He is very proud of it, as all good engines are – but he doesn't mind the rain now, because he knows that the best way to keep his paint nice is not to run into tunnels, but to ask his Driver to rub him down when the day's work is over.

Henry and the Elephant

ILLUSTRATED BY C. REGINALD DALBY

HENRY and Gordon were lonely when Thomas left the Yard to run his branch line. They missed him very much.

They had more work to do. They couldn't wait in the Shed till it was time, and find their coaches at the platform; they had to fetch them. They didn't like that.

Edward sometimes did odd jobs, and so did James, but James soon started grumbling too. The Fat Controller kindly gave Henry and Gordon new coats of paint (Henry chose green), but they still grumbled dreadfully.

"We get no rest, we get no rest," they complained as they clanked about the Yard; but the coaches only laughed.

"You're lazy and slack, you're lazy and slack," they answered in their quiet, rude way.

But when a Circus came to town, the engines forgot they were tired. They all wanted to shunt the special trucks and coaches.

They were dreadfully jealous of James when the Fat Controller told him to pull the train when the Circus went away.

However, they soon forgot about the animals as they had plenty of work to do.

One morning Henry was told to take some workmen to a tunnel which was blocked.

He grumbled away to find two trucks to carry the workmen and their tools.

"Pushing trucks! Pushing trucks!" he muttered in a sulky sort of way.

They stopped outside the tunnel, and tried to look through it, but it was quite dark; no daylight shone from the other end.

The workmen took their tools and went inside.

Suddenly with a shout they all ran out looking frightened.

"We went to the block and started to dig, but it grunted and moved," they said.

"Rubbish," said the foreman.

"It's not rubbish, it's big and alive; we're not going in there again."

"Right," said the foreman, "I'll ride in a truck and Henry shall push it out."

"Wheeeesh," said Henry unhappily. He hated tunnels (he had been shut up in one once), but this was worse; something big and alive was inside.

"Peep peep peep pip pip pee — eep!" he whistled, "I don't want to go in!"

"Neither do I," said his Driver, "but we must clear the line."

"Oh dear! Oh dear!" puffed Henry as they slowly advanced into the darkness.

B U M P —————— ! ! ! !

Henry's Driver shut off steam at once.

"Help! Help! We're going back," wailed Henry, and slowly moving out into the daylight came first Henry, then the trucks, and last of all, pushing hard and rather cross, came a large elephant.

"Well I never did!" said the foreman. "It's an elephant from the Circus."

Henry's Driver put on his brakes, and a man ran to telephone for the keeper.

The elephant stopped pushing and came towards them. They gave him some sandwiches and cake, so he forgot he was cross and remembered he was hungry. He drank three buckets of water without stopping, and

was just going to drink another when Henry let off steam.

The elephant jumped, and "hoo —— oosh", he squirted the water over Henry by mistake.

Poor Henry!

When the keeper came, the workmen rode home happily in the trucks, laughing at their adventure, but Henry was very cross.

"An elephant pushed me! an elephant hooshed me!" he hissed.

He was sulky all day, and his coaches had an uncomfortable time.

In the Shed he told Gordon and James about the elephant, and I am sorry to say that instead of laughing and telling him not to be silly, they looked sad and said:

"You poor engine, you have been badly treated."

COAL

ILLUSTRATED BY C. REGINALD DALBY

"I SUFFER dreadfully, and no one cares."

"Rubbish, Henry," snorted James, "you don't work hard enough."

Henry was bigger than James, but smaller than Gordon. Sometimes he could pull trains; sometimes he had no strength at all.

The Fat Controller spoke to him too. "You are too expensive, Henry. You have had lots of new parts and new paint too, but they've done you no good. If we can't make you better, we must get another engine instead of you."

This made Henry, his Driver, and his Fireman very sad.

The Fat Controller was waiting when Henry came to the platform. He had taken off his hat and coat, and put on overalls.

He climbed to the footplate and Henry started.

"Henry is a 'bad steamer'," said the Fireman. "I build up his fire, but it doesn't give enough heat."

Henry tried very hard, but it was no good. He had not enough steam, and they stopped outside Edward's station.

"Oh dear!" thought Henry sadly, "I shall have to go away."

Edward took charge of the train. Henry stopped behind.

"What do you think is wrong, Fireman?" asked the Fat Controller.

The Fireman mopped his face. "Excuse me, Sir," he answered, "but the coal is wrong. We've had a poor lot lately, and today it's worse. The other engines can manage; they have big fireboxes. Henry's is small and can't make the heat. With Welsh coal he'd be a different engine."

"It's expensive," said the Fat Controller thoughtfully, "but Henry must have a fair chance. James shall go and fetch some."

When the Welsh coal came, Henry's Driver and Fireman were excited.

"Now we'll show them, Henry old fellow!" They carefully oiled all his joints and polished his brass till it shone like gold.

His fire had already been lit, so the Fireman "made it" carefully.

He put large lumps of coal like a wall round the outside. Then he covered the glowing middle part with smaller lumps.

"You're spoiling my fire," complained Henry.

"Wait and see," said the Fireman. "We'll have a roaring fire just when we want it."

He was right. When Henry reached the platform, the water was boiling nicely, and he had to let off steam, to show how

happy he was. He made such a noise that the Fat Controller came out to see him.

"How are you, Henry?"

"Pip peep peep!" whistled Henry, "I feel fine!"

"Have you a good fire, Driver?"

"Never better Sir, *and* plenty of steam."

"No record breaking," warned the Fat Controller, smiling. "Don't push him too hard."

"Henry won't need pushing, Sir; I'll have to hold him back."

Henry had a lovely day. He had never felt so well in his life. He wanted to go fast, but his Driver wouldn't let him. "Steady old fellow," he would say, "there's plenty of time."

They arrived early at the junction.

"Where have you been, lazybones?" asked Henry, when Thomas puffed in, "I can't wait for dawdling tank engines like you! Goodbye!"

"Whoooosh!" said Thomas to Annie and Clarabel as Henry disappeared, "have you ever seen anything like it?"

Both Annie and Clarabel agreed that they never had.

THE FLYING KIPPER

ILLUSTRATED BY C. REGINALD DALBY

Lots of ships use the harbour at the Big Station by the sea. The passenger ships have spotless paint and shining brass. Other ships, though smaller and dirtier, are important too. They take coal, machinery and other things abroad, and bring back meat, timber and things we need.

Fishing boats also come there. They unload their fish on the quay. Some of it is sent to shops in the town, and some goes in a special train to other places far away.

The railwaymen call this train "The Flying Kipper".

One winter evening Henry's Driver said: "We'll be out early tomorrow. We've got to take 'The Flying Kipper'."

"Don't tell Gordon," he whispered, "but I think if we pull the 'Kipper' nicely, the Fat Controller will let us pull the Express."

"Hurrah!" cried Henry, excited. "That will be lovely."

He was ready at 5 o'clock. There was snow and frost. Men hustled and shouted, loading the vans with crates of fish. The last door banged, the Guard showed his green lamp, and they were off.

"Come on! Come on! dontbesilly! — dontbesilly!" puffed Henry to the vans, as his wheels slipped on the icy rails.

The vans shuddered and groaned. "Trock, Trick, Trock, Trick; all right, all right," they answered grudgingly.

"That is better, that is better," puffed Henry more happily, as the train began to gather speed.

Thick clouds of smoke and steam poured from his funnel into the cold air; and when his Fireman put on more coal, the fire's light shone brightly on the snow around.

"Hurry, hurry, hurry," panted Henry.

They hooshed under bridges, and clattered through stations, green signal-lights showing as they passed.

They were going well, the light grew better and a yellow signal appeared ahead.

"Distant signal – up," thought Henry, "caution." His Driver, shutting off steam, prepared to stop, but the home signal was down. "All clear, Henry; away we go."

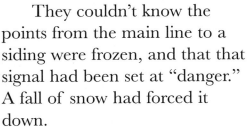

They couldn't know the points from the main line to a siding were frozen, and that that signal had been set at "danger." A fall of snow had forced it down.

A goods train waited in the siding to let "The Flying Kipper" pass. The Driver and Fireman were drinking cocoa in the brake van.

The Guard pulled out his watch. "The 'Kipper' is due," he said.

"Who cares?" said the Fireman. "This is good cocoa."

The Driver got up, "Come on Fireman, back to our engine."

"Hey!" the Fireman grumbled, "I haven't finished my cocoa yet."

A sudden crash – the brake van broke – the three men shot in the air like Jacks-in-the-box, and landed in the snow outside.

Henry's Driver and the Fireman jumped clear before the crash. The Fireman fell head first into a heap of snow. He kicked so hard that the Driver couldn't pull him out.

Henry sprawled on his side. He looked surprised. The goods train Fireman waved his empty mug.

"You clumsy great engine! The best cup of cocoa I've ever had, and you bump into me and spill it all!"

"Never mind your cocoa, Fireman," laughed his Driver, "run and telephone the breakdown gang."

The gang soon cleared the line, but they had hard work lifting Henry to the rails.

The Fat Controller came to see him.

"The signal was down, Sir," said Henry nervously.

"Cheer up, Henry! It wasn't your fault. Ice and snow caused the accident. I'm sending you to Crewe, a fine place for sick engines. They'll give you a new shape and a larger firebox. Then you'll feel a different engine, and won't need special coal any more. Won't that be nice?"

"Yes, Sir," said Henry doubtfully.

Henry liked being at Crewe, but was glad to come home.

A crowd of people waited to see him arrive in his new shape. He looked so splendid and strong that they gave him three cheers.

"Peep peep pippippeep! Thank you very much," he whistled happily.

I am sorry to say that a lot of little boys are often late for school because they wait to see Henry go by!

They often see him pulling the Express; and he does it so well that Gordon is jealous. But that is another story.

GORDON'S WHISTLE

ILLUSTRATED BY C. REGINALD DALBY

GORDON was cross.

"Why should Henry have a new shape?" he grumbled. "A shape good enough for ME is good enough for him. He goes gallivanting off to Crewe, leaving us to do his work. It's disgraceful!"

"And there's another thing. Henry whistles too much. No *respectable* engine ever whistles loudly at stations."

"It isn't wrong," said Gordon, "but we just don't do it."

Poor Henry didn't feel happy any more.

"Never mind," whispered Percy, "I'm glad you are home again; I like your whistling."

"Goodbye, Henry," called Gordon next morning as he left the Shed. "We are glad to have you with us again, but be sure and remember what I said about whistling."

Later on Henry took a slow train, and presently stopped at Edward's station.

"Hullo Henry," said

Edward, "you look splendid; I was pleased to hear your happy whistle yesterday."

"Thank you, Edward," smiled Henry . . . "Sh Sh! Can you hear something?"

Edward listened – far away, but getting louder and louder, was the sound of an engine's whistle.

"It sounds like Gordon," said Edward, "and it ought to be Gordon, but Gordon never whistles like that."

It *was* Gordon.

He came rushing down the hill at a tremendous rate. He didn't look at Henry, and he didn't look at Edward; he was purple in the boiler, and whistling fit to burst.

He screamed through the station and disappeared.

"Well!!!" said Edward, looking at Henry.

"It isn't wrong," chuckled Henry, "but we just don't do it," and he told Edward what Gordon had said.

Meanwhile Gordon screeched along the line. People came out of their houses, air-raid sirens started, five fire brigades got ready to go out, horses upset their carts, and old ladies dropped their parcels.

At a Big Station the noise was awful. Porters and passengers held their ears. The Fat Controller held his ears too; he gave a lot of orders, but no one could hear them, and

Gordon went on whistling. At last he clambered into Gordon's cab.

"Take him away," he bellowed, "**AND STOP THAT NOISE!**"

Still whistling, Gordon puffed sadly away.

He whistled as he crossed the points; he whistled on the siding; he was still whistling as the last deafened passenger left the station.

Then two fitters climbed up and knocked his whistle valve into place ——— —— and there was SILENCE.

Gordon slunk into the Shed. He was glad it was empty.

The others came in later. "It isn't wrong," murmured Henry to no one in particular, "but we just don't do it."

No one mentioned whistles!

Henry's Sneeze

Illustrated by C. Reginald Dalby

ONE lovely Saturday morning, Henry was puffing along. The sun shone, the fields were green, the birds sang; Henry had plenty of steam in his boiler, and he was feeling happy.

"I feel so well, I feel so well," he sang.

"Trickety trock, Trickety trock," hummed his coaches.

Henry saw some boys on a bridge.

"Peep! Peep! Hullo!" he whistled cheerfully.

"Peep! Peep! Peeeep!" he called the next moment. "Oh! Oh! Oooh!" For the boys didn't wave and take his number; they dropped stones on him instead.

They were silly, stupid boys who thought it would be fun to drop stones down his funnel. Some of the stones hit Henry's boiler and spoilt his paint; one hit the Fireman on the head as he was shovelling coal, and others broke the carriage windows.

"It's a shame, it's a shame," hissed Henry.

"They've broken our glass, they've broken our glass," sobbed the coaches.

The Driver opened the first-aid box, bandaged the Fireman's head, and planned what he was going to do.

They stopped the train and the Guard asked if any passengers were hurt. No one was hurt, but everyone was cross. They saw the Fireman's bumped head, and told him what to do for it, and they looked at Henry's paint.

"Call the Police," they shouted angrily.

"No!" said the Driver, "leave it to Henry and me. We'll teach those lads a lesson."

"What will you do?" they asked.

"Can you keep a secret?"

"Yes, yes," they all said.

"Well then," said the Driver, "Henry is going to sneeze at them."

"What!" cried all the passengers.

The Driver laughed.

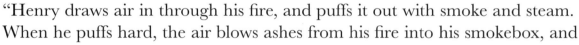

"Henry draws air in through his fire, and puffs it out with smoke and steam. When he puffs hard, the air blows ashes from his fire into his smokebox, and these ashes sometimes prevent him puffing properly.

"When your nose is blocked, you sometimes sneeze. If Henry's smoke box is blocked, I can make air and steam blow the ashes out through his funnel.

"We will do it at the bridge and startle those boys."

Henry puffed on to the terminus, where he had a rest. Then he took the train back. Lots of people were waiting at the station just before the bridge. They wanted to see what would happen.

"Henry has plenty of ashes," said the Driver. "Please keep all windows shut till we have passed the bridge. Henry is as excited as we are, aren't you old fellow?" and he patted Henry's boiler.

Henry didn't answer; he was feeling "stuffed up", but he winked at his Driver, like this.

The Guard's flag waved, his whistle blew, and they were off. Soon in the distance they saw the bridge. There were the boys, and they all had stones.

"Are you ready, Henry?" said his Driver. "Sneeze hard when I tell you."

"NOW!" he said, and turned the handle.

"Atisha Atisha Atishoooooh!"

Smoke and steam and ashes spouted from his funnel. They went all over the bridge, and all over the boys who ran away as black as soot.

"Well done, Henry," laughed his Driver, "they won't drop stones on engines again."

"Your coat is all black, but we'll rub you down and paint your scratches and you'll be as good as new tomorrow."

Henry has never again sneezed under a bridge. The Fat Controller doesn't like it. His smoke box is always cleaned in the Yard while he is resting.

He has now gone under more bridges than he can count; but from that day to this there have been no more boys with stones.

TENDERS FOR HENRY

ILLUSTRATED BY GUNVOR AND PETER EDWARDS

"I'M not happy," complained Gordon.

"Your fire box is out of order," said James. "No wonder, after all that coal you had yesterday."

"Hard work brings good appetite," snapped Gordon. "*You* wouldn't understand."

"I know," put in Duck, brightly. "It's boiler-ache. I warned you about that standpipe on the Other Railway; but you drank gallons."

"It's *not* boiler-ache," protested Gordon. "It's . . ."

"Of course it is," said Henry. "That water's bad. It furs up your tubes. Your boiler must be full of sludge. Have a good wash-out. Then, you'll feel a different engine."

"Don't be vulgar," said Gordon huffily.

Gordon backed down on his train, hissing mournfully.

"Cheer up, Gordon!" said the Fat Controller.

"I can't, Sir. The others say I've got boiler-ache, but I haven't, Sir. I keep thinking about the Dreadful State of the World, Sir. Is it true, Sir, what the diesels say?"

"What do they say?"

"They boast that they've *abolished Steam*, Sir."

"Yes, Gordon. It is true."

"What, Sir! All my Doncaster brothers, drawn the same time as me?"

"All gone, except one."

The Guard's whistle blew, and Gordon puffed sadly away.

"Poor old Gordon!" said the Fat Controller. "Hmm . . . If only we could! . . . Yes, I'll ask his Owner at once." He hurried away.

Arrangements took time, but one evening, Gordon's Driver ran back, excited. "Wake up, Gordon! The Fat Controller's given you a surprise. Look!"

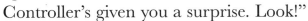

Gordon could hardly believe it. Backing towards him were two massive green tenders, and their engine's shape was very like his own. "It's Flying Scotsman!" he gasped. "The Fat Controller's brought him to see me. Oh thank you, Sir!"

Gordon's toot of joy was drowned by Flying Scotsman's as he drew happily alongside.

Next day the two engines were photographed side by side.

"You've changed a lot," smiled Flying Scotsman.

"I had a 'rebuild' at Crewe. They didn't do a proper Doncaster job, of course, but it serves."

"I had a 'rebuild' too, and looked hideous. But my Owner said I was an Extra Special Engine, and made them give me back my proper shape."

"Is that why you have two tenders, being Special?"

"No. You'd hardly believe it, Gordon, but Over There, they've hardly *any coal and water.*"

"But surely, every *proper* railway . . ."

"Exactly. You are lucky, Gordon, to have a Controller who knows how to run railways."

Everyone got on well with Flying Scotsman except Henry. Henry was jealous.

"Tenders are marks of distinction," he complained. "Everybody knows that. Why's he got two?"

"He's famous," explained Duck and Donald. "He was the second to go 100 miles an hour; besides, the Other Railway has no coal and water."

"Pooh!" sniffed Henry. "I can't believe *that*! I never boast," he continued, "but I always work hard enough for two. I deserve another tender for that."

Duck whispered something to Donald.

"Henry," asked Duck innocently, "would you like *my* tenders?"

"Yours!" exclaimed Henry. "What have *you* got to do with tenders?"

"All right," said Duck. "The deal's off. Would you like them Donald?"

"I wudna deprive ye of the honour."

"It *is* a great honour," said Duck, thoughtfully, "but I'm only a tank engine, so I don't really understand tenders. Perhaps James might . . ."

"I'm sorry I was rude," said Henry hastily. "How many tenders have you, and when could I have them?"

"Six, and you can have them this evening."

"Six lovely tenders," chortled Henry. "What a splendid sight I'll be! That'll show the others the sort of engine I am!"

Henry was excited. "D'you think it'll be all right?" he asked for the umpteenth time.

"Of course," said Duck. "Just go where I told you, and they'll all be ready."

Meanwhile, word had gone round, and the others waited where they could get a good view. Henry was cheered to the echo when he came, but he wasn't a splendid sight. He had six tenders, true, but they were very old and very dirty. All were filled with boiler sludge!

"Had a good wash-out, Henry?" called a voice. "That's right. You feel a different engine now." Henry was not sure, but he thought the voice was Gordon's.

SUPER RESCUE

ILLUSTRATED BY GUNVOR AND PETER EDWARDS

THE two diesels surveyed the Shed. "It's time, 7101," said one, "that we took this railway over."

"Shsh, 199! It's *their* railway, after all."

"Not for long," persisted 199. "Our Controller says, 'Steam engines spoil our Image'."

"Of course we do," snapped Duck. "We show what frauds you are. Call yourselves engines? If anything happens, *you* care nothing for your train. *You* just moan for a Fitter. *We* bring it home, if only on one cylinder."

"Nothing," boasted 199, "*ever* happens to us. *We* are reliable."

Vulgar noises greeted this.

"How rude!" said 199.

"You asked for it," growled 7101. "Now shut up!"

Next day, Henry was rolling home, tenderfirst. "I'm a 'failed engine'," he moaned. "Lost my regulator – Driver says it's jammed wide open, and he can't mend it till I'm cool."

"However," he went on, "I've got steam, and Driver can use my reverser; but it *would* happen after Duck fooled me with those tenders. Now they'll laugh at me again."

He reached a signal box and stopped, whistling for a "road".

Opposite the box, on the "up" line, stood diesel 199 with a train of oil-tankers.

"Worse and worse," thought Henry. "Now 'Old Reliable' will laugh at me, too."

The Signalman came out. "For pity's sake take this Spamcan away. It's failed. The 'Limited' is behind, and all he does is wail for his Fitter."

"Spamcan!" fumed 199. "I'm . . ."

"Stow it!" snapped the Signalman, "or I'll take my tin-opener to you. Now then!"

199 subsided at this dreadful threat, and Henry pulled the train out of the way. The diesel didn't help. He just sulked.

The "Limited" rushed by with a growl and a roar. Henry gave a chuckle. "Look, Spamcan," he said. "There's your little pal."

The diesel said nothing. He hoped 7101 hadn't noticed.

7101 hadn't noticed. He had troubles of his own. He was cross with his coaches. They seemed to be getting heavier. He roared at them, but it did no good.

Engines have a pump called an ejector which draws air out of the train's brake pipes to keep the brakes "off". If it fails, air leaks in and the brakes come "on", gently at first, then harder and harder.

7101's ejector had failed. The brakes were already "leaking on" while he passed Henry. He struggled on for half a mile before being brought to a stand, growling furiously, unable to move a wheel.

"Well! Well! Well! Did you hear what Signalman said?"

"I thought they'd be laughing at me!" chuckled Henry. "Now, the joke's on them!"

"Moving two 'dead' diesels and their trains?" said his Driver thoughtfully. "That's no joke for a 'failed' engine. D'you think you can do it?"

"I'll have a good try," said Henry with spirit. "Anyway, 7101's better than old Spamcan. He did try and shut him up last night."

"Come on, then," said his Driver. "We mustn't keep the passengers waiting."

"GET MOV – ING YOU!" Henry puffed the sulky diesel into motion, and started to the rescue.

Henry gently buffered up to the Express. While the two Drivers talked, his Fireman joined his front brake-pipe to the coaches.

"It's better than we thought, Henry," said his Driver. "The diesel can pull if we keep the brakes 'off'. So the only weight we'll have is Spamcan's goods."

"Whoosh!" said Henry. "That's a mercy." He was, by now, feeling rather puffed.

"Poop poop poopoop! Are you ready?" tooted 7101.

"Peep peep peeeep! Yes I am!" whistled Henry.

So, with 7101 growling in front, and Henry gamely puffing in the middle, the long cavalcade set out for the next Big Station.

Donald and Flying Scotsman were waiting. They cheered as Henry puffed past.

He braked the coaches thankfully; Spamcan and the tankers trailed far behind.

The passengers buzzed out like angry bees; but the Fat Controller told them about Henry, so they forgot to be cross and thanked Henry instead. They called him an Enterprising Engine, and took his photograph.

They were thrilled too, when Flying Scotsman backed down on their train. If the Guard hadn't tactfully "shooed" them to their coaches the train would have started later than ever.

Donald took the "goods". "Return 199 to the Other Railway," ordered the Fat Controller. "I will write my views later."

Henry and 7101 went away together.

"I'm sorry about last night," ventured the diesel.

"That's all right. You did shut 'Old Reliable' up."

"And," said the diesel ruefully, "made a fool of myself today too."

"Rubbish! A failed ejector might happen to anyone. I'd lost my regulator."

"You! Failed?" exclaimed the diesel. "And yet . . ." His voice trailed away in admiration.

"Well!" said Henry. "Emergency, you know. Trains *must* get through."

7101 said no more. He had a lot to think about.

JAMES
the Red Engine

In which James has trouble

with a top hat, some bootlaces

and a beehive . . .

JAMES AND THE TOP HAT

ILLUSTRATED BY C. REGINALD DALBY

JAMES was a new engine who lived at a station at the other end of the line. He had two small wheels in front and six driving wheels behind. They weren't as big as Gordon's, and they weren't as small as Thomas'.

"You're a special Mixed-Traffic engine," the Fat Controller told him. "You'll be able to pull coaches or trucks quite easily."

But trucks are not easy things to manage and on his first day they had pushed him down a hill into a field.

He had been ill after the accident, but now he had new brakes and a shining coat of red paint.

"The red paint will cheer you up after your accident," said the Fat Controller kindly. "You are to pull coaches today, and Edward shall help you."

They went together to find the coaches.

"Be careful with the coaches, James," said Edward, "they don't like being bumped. Trucks are silly and noisy; they need to be bumped and taught to behave, but coaches get cross and will pay you out."

They took the coaches to the platform and were both coupled on in front. The Fat Controller, the Stationmaster, and some little boys all came to admire James' shining rods and red paint.

James was pleased. "I am a really splendid engine," he thought, and

suddenly let off steam. "Whee —
ee — ee — ee — eesh!"

The Fat Controller, the
Stationmaster and the Guard all
jumped, and a shower of water
fell on the Fat Controller's nice
new top-hat.

Just then the whistle blew
and James thought they had
better go – so they went!

"Go on, go on," he puffed
to Edward.

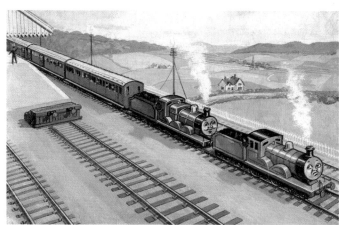

"Don't push, don't push,"
puffed Edward, for he did not
like starting quickly.

"Don't go so fast, don't go
so fast," grumbled the coaches;
but James did not listen. He
wanted to run away before the
Fat Controller could call him
back.

He didn't even want to stop
at the first station. Edward tried

hard to stop, but the two
coaches in front were beyond
the platform before they
stopped, and they had to go
back to let the passengers get
out.

Lots of people came to look
at James, and, as no one seemed
to know about the Fat
Controller's top-hat, James felt
happier.

Presently they came to the junction where Thomas was waiting with his two coaches.

"Hullo, James!" said Thomas kindly, "feeling better? That's right. Ah! That's my Guard's whistle. I must go. Sorry I can't stop. I don't know what the Fat Controller would do without me to run this branch line," and he puffed off importantly with his two coaches into a tunnel.

Leaving the junction, they passed the field where James had had his accident. The fence was mended and the cows were back again. James whistled, but they paid no attention.

They clattered through Edward's station yard and started to climb the hill beyond.

"It's ever so steep, it's ever so steep," puffed James.

"I've done it before, I've done it before," puffed Edward.

"It's steep, but we'll do it – it's steep, but we'll do it," the two engines puffed together as they pulled the train up the long hill.

They both rested at the next station; Edward told James how Gordon had stuck on the hill, and he had had to push him up!

James laughed so much that he got hiccoughs and surprised an old lady in a black bonnet.

She dropped all her parcels, and three porters, the Stationmaster and the Guard had to run after her picking them up!

James was quiet in the Shed that night. He had enjoyed his day, but he was a little afraid of what the Fat Controller would say about the top-hat!

JAMES AND THE BOOTLACE

ILLUSTRATED BY C. REGINALD DALBY

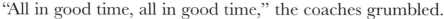

NEXT morning the Fat Controller spoke severely to James: "If you can't behave, I shall take away your red coat and have you painted blue."

James did not like that at all and he was very rough with the coaches as he brought them to the platform.

"Come along, come along," he called rudely.

"All in good time, all in good time," the coaches grumbled.

"Don't talk, come on!" answered James, and with the coaches squealing and grumbling after him, he snorted into the station.

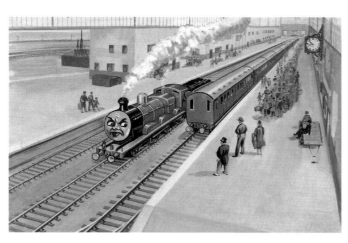

James *was* cross that morning. The Fat Controller had spoken to him, the coaches had dawdled and, worst of all, he had had to fetch his own coaches.

"Gordon never does," thought James, "and he is only painted blue. A splendid Red Engine like me should never have to fetch his own coaches." And he puffed and snorted round to the front of the train, and backed on to it with a rude bump.

"O — ooooh!" groaned the coaches, "that was too bad!"

To make James even more cross, he then had to take the coaches to a different platform, where no one came near him as he stood there. The Fat Controller was in his office, the Stationmaster was at the other end of the train with the Guard, and even the little boys stood a long way off.

James felt lonely. "I'll show them!" he said to himself. "They think

Gordon is the only engine who can pull coaches."

And as soon as the Guard's whistle blew, he started off with a tremendous jerk.

"Come on! — come on! — come on!" he puffed, and the coaches, squeaking and groaning in protest, clattered over the points on to the open line.

"Hurry! — hurry! — hurry!" puffed James.

"You're going too fast, you're going too fast," said the coaches, and indeed they were going so fast that they swayed from side to side.

James laughed and tried to go faster, but the coaches wouldn't let him.

"We're going to stop — we're going to stop — we're — going — to — stop," they said

and James found himself going slower and slower.

"What's the matter?" James asked his Driver.

"The brakes are hard on – leak in the pipe most likely. You've banged the coaches enough to make a leak in anything."

The Guard and the Driver got down and looked at the

brake pipes all along the train.

At last they found a hole where rough treatment had made a joint work loose.

"How shall we mend it?" said the Guard.

James' Driver thought for a moment.

"We'll do it with newspapers and a leather bootlace."

"Well, where is the bootlace coming from?" asked the Guard. "We haven't one."

"Ask the passengers," said the Driver.

So the Guard made everyone get out.

"Has anybody got a leather bootlace?" he asked.

They all said "No" except one man in a bowler hat (whose name was Jeremiah Jobling) who tried to hide his feet.

"You have a leather bootlace there I see, sir," said the Guard. "Please give it to me."

"I won't," said Jeremiah Jobling.

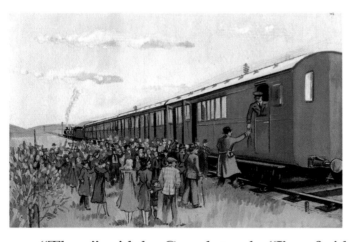

"Then," said the Guard sternly, "I'm afraid this train will just stop where it is."

Then the passengers all told the Guard, the Driver and the Fireman what a Bad Railway it was. But the Guard climbed into his van, and the Driver and Fireman made James let off steam. So they all told Jeremiah Jobling he was a Bad Man instead.

At last he gave them his laces, the Driver tied a pad of newspapers tightly round the hole, and James was able to pull the train.

But he was a sadder and a wiser James and took care never to bump coaches again.

TROUBLESOME TRUCKS

ILLUSTRATED BY C. REGINALD DALBY

JAMES did not see the Fat Controller for several days. They left James alone in the shed, and did not even allow him to go out and push coaches and trucks in the Yard.

"Oh, dear!" he thought sadly, "I'll never be allowed out any more; I shall have to stay in this shed for always, and no one will ever see my red coat again. Oh, dear! Oh, dear!" James began to cry.

Just then the Fat Controller came along.

"I see you are sorry, James," he said. "I hope, now, that you will be a better Engine. You have given me a lot of trouble. People are laughing at my Railway, and I do not like that at all."

"I am very sorry, Sir," said James. "I will try hard to behave."

"That's a good engine," said the Fat Controller kindly. "I want you to pull some trucks for me. Run along and find them."

So James puffed happily away.

"Here are your trucks, James," said a little tank engine. "Have you got some bootlaces ready?" And he ran off laughing rudely.

"Oh! Oh! Oh!" said the trucks, as James backed down on them. "We want a proper engine, not a Red Monster."

James took no notice and started as soon as the Guard was ready.

"Come along, come along," he puffed.

"We won't! We won't!" screamed the trucks.

But James didn't care, and he pulled the screeching trucks sternly out of the yard.

The trucks tried hard to make him give up, but he still kept on.

Sometimes their brakes would slip "on", and sometimes their axles would "run hot".

pulled them along the line.

At last they saw Gordon's Hill ahead.

"Look out for trouble, James," warned his Driver. "We'll go fast and get them up before they know it. Don't let them stop you."

So James went faster, and they were soon halfway up the hill.

"I'm doing it! I'm doing it!" he panted.

Each time they would have to stop and put the trouble right and each time James would start again, determined not to let the trucks beat him.

"Give up! Give up! You can't pull us! You can't! You can't!" called the trucks.

"I can and I will! I can and I will!" puffed James.

And slowly but surely he

But it was hard work.

"Will the top never come?" he thought, when with a sudden jerk it all came easier.

"I've done it! I've done it!" he puffed triumphantly.

"Hurrah!" he thought, "it's easy now." But his Driver shut off steam.

"They've done it again," he said. "We've left our tail behind!"

The last ten trucks were running backwards down the hill. The coupling had snapped!

But the Guard was brave. Very carefully and cleverly he made them stop. Then he got out and walked down the line with his red flag.

"That's why it was easy," said James as he backed the other trucks carefully down. "What silly things trucks are! There might have been an accident."

Meanwhile the Guard had stopped Edward who was pulling three coaches.

"Shall I help you, James?" called Edward.

"No, thank you," answered James, "I'll pull them myself."

"Good, don't let them beat you."

So James got ready. Then with a "peep, peep" he was off.

"I *can* do it, I *can* do it," he puffed. He pulled and puffed as hard as he could.

"Peep pip peep peep! You're doing well!" whistled Edward, as James slowly struggled up the hill, with clouds of smoke and steam pouring from his funnel.

"I've done it, I've done it," he panted and disappeared over the top.

They reached their station safely. James was resting in the yard, when Edward puffed by with a cheerful "peep peep".

Then, walking towards him across the rails, James saw . . . the Fat Controller!

"Oh dear! What will he say?" he asked himself sadly.

But the Fat Controller was smiling. "I was in Edward's train, and saw everything," he said. "You've made the most troublesome trucks on the line behave. After that, you deserve to keep your red coat."

JAMES AND THE EXPRESS

ILLUSTRATED BY C. REGINALD DALBY

SOMETIMES Gordon and Henry slept in James' shed, and they would talk of nothing but bootlaces! James would talk about engines who got shut up in tunnels and stuck on hills, but they wouldn't listen, and went on talking and laughing.

"You talk too much, little James," Gordon would say. "A fine strong engine like me has something to talk about. I'm the only engine who can pull the Express. When I'm not there, they need two engines. Think of that!

"I've pulled expresses for years, and have never once lost my way. I seem to know the right line by instinct," said Gordon proudly. Every wise engine knows, of course, that the Signalman works the points to make engines run on the right lines, but Gordon was so proud that he had forgotten.

"Wake up, James," he said next morning, "it's nearly time for the Express. What are you doing? – Odd jobs? Ah well! We all have to begin somewhere, don't we? Run along now and get my coaches – don't be late now."

James went to get Gordon's coaches. They were now all shining with lovely new paint. He was careful not to bump them, and they followed him smoothly into the station singing happily. "We're going away, we're going away."

"I wish I was going with you," said James. "I should love to pull the Express and go flying along the line."

He left them in the station and went back to the yard, just as Gordon with much noise and blowing of steam backed on to the train.

The Fat Controller was on the train with other Important People, and, as soon as they heard the Guard's whistle, Gordon started.

"Look at me now! Look at me now!" he puffed, and the coaches glided after him out of the station.

"Poop poop poo poo poop! — Good-bye little James! See you tomorrow."

James watched the train disappear round a curve, and then went back to work. He pushed some trucks into their proper sidings and went to fetch the coaches for another train.

He brought the coaches to the platform and was just being

uncoupled when he heard a mournful, quiet "Shush shush shush shush!" and there was Gordon trying to sidle into the station without being noticed.

"Hullo, Gordon! Is it tomorrow?" asked James. Gordon didn't answer; he just let off steam feebly.

"Did you lose your way, Gordon?"

"No, it was lost for me," he answered crossly, "I was switched off the main line on to the loop; I had to go all round and back again."

"Perhaps it was instinct," said James brightly.

Meanwhile all the passengers hurried to the booking office. "We want our money back," they shouted.

Everyone was making a noise, but the Fat Controller climbed on a trolley and blew the Guard's whistle so loudly that they all stopped to look at him.

Then he promised them a new train at once.

"Gordon can't do it," he said. "Will you pull it for us, James?"

"Yes, sir, I'll try."

So James was coupled on and everyone got in again.

"Do your best, James," said the Fat Controller kindly. Just then the whistle blew and he had to run to get in.

"Come along, come along," puffed James.

"You're pulling us well! You're pulling us well," sang the coaches.

"Hurry, hurry, hurry," puffed James.

Stations and bridges flashed by, the passengers leaned out of the windows and cheered, and they soon reached the terminus.

Everyone said "Thank you" to James. "Well done," said the Fat Controller. "Would you like to pull the Express sometimes?"

"Yes, please," answered James happily.

Next day when James came by, Gordon was pushing trucks in the Yard.

"I like some quiet work for a change," he said. "I'm teaching these trucks manners. You did well with those coaches I hear . . . good, we'll show them!" and he gave his trucks a bump, making them cry, "Oh! Oh! Oh! Oh!"

James and Gordon are now good friends. James sometimes takes the Express to give Gordon a rest. Gordon never talks about bootlaces, and they are both quite agreed on the subject of trucks!

Buzz Buzz

ILLUSTRATED BY GUNVOR AND PETER EDWARDS

BoCo reached the Big Station and arranged his trucks. Then he went to the Shed, and asked politely if he could come in.

Duck was not pleased to see a diesel but, presently, when he found that BoCo knew Edward, he became more friendly. And by the time BoCo had told him about Bill and Ben they were laughing together like old friends.

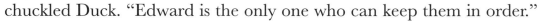

"Have they ever played tricks on *you?*" asked BoCo.

"Goodness me! Yes!" chuckled Duck. "Edward is the only one who can keep them in order."

"You know," went on Duck, "I sometimes call them 'The Bees'."

"A good name," chuckled BoCo. "They're terrors when they start buzzing round."

Just then James bustled in. "What's that, Duck? Are you terrified of bees? They're only insects after all: so don't let that buzz-box diesel tell you different."

"His name is BoCo, and he didn't. We . . . "

"I wouldn't care," interrupted James, "if hundreds were swarming round. I'd just blow smoke and make them buzz off."

"Buzz Buzz Buzz," retorted Duck.

James retired into a huff.

James was to pull the Express next morning, and when Duck brought his coaches the platform was crowded.

"Mind your backs! MIND YOUR BACKS!" Two porters were taking a loaded trolley to the front van. Fred drove, while Bert walked behind.

"Careful, Fred! Careful!" warned Bert, but Fred was in a hurry and didn't listen.

Suddenly an old lady appeared in front.

Fred stopped dead, but the luggage slid forward and burst the lid of a large white wooden box.

Some bees flew out, and, just as James came backing down, they began to explore the station.

Someone shouted a warning. The platform cleared like magic.

The bees were too sleepy to be cross. They found the empty station cold. James' Fireman was trying to couple the train. They buzzed round him hopefully. They wanted him to mend their hive. Then they could go back and be warm again.

But the Fireman didn't understand. He thought they would sting him.

He gave a yell, ran back to the cab and crouched with his jacket over his head.

The Driver didn't understand either. He swatted at the bees with the shovel.

The bees, disappointed, turned their attention to James.

James' boiler was nice and warm. The bees swarmed round it happily.

"Buzz off! BUZZ OFF!" he hissed. He made smoke, but the wind blew it away, and the bees stayed.

At last one settled on his hot smokebox. It burnt its feet. The bee thought James had stung it on purpose. It stung James back – right on the nose!

"Eeeeeeeeeeeee!" whistled James. He had had enough: so had his Driver and Fireman. They started without waiting for the Guard's whistle.

They didn't notice till too late, that they'd left their train behind.

In the end it was BoCo who pulled the Express. He was worried at first about leaving his trucks, but Duck promised to look after them and so it was arranged. He managed to gain back some of the lost time, and the Fat Controller was pleased with him.

No one seemed to notice when James came back to the Shed. They were talking about a new kind of beehive on wheels. It was red, they said. Then they all said "Buzz, buzz, buzz," and laughed a lot.

James thought that for big Main Line Engines they were being very silly.